Hawaii

(Alicia Myles #6)

By
David Leadbeater

Classification: Thriller, adventure, action, mystery,
suspense, archaeological, military, historical,
assassination, terrorism, assassin, spy

Other Books by David Leadbeater:

The Matt Drake Series
A constantly evolving, action-packed romp based in
the escapist action-adventure genre:

The Bones of Odin (Matt Drake #1)
The Blood King Conspiracy (Matt Drake #2)
The Gates of Hell (Matt Drake 3)
The Tomb of the Gods (Matt Drake #4)
Brothers in Arms (Matt Drake #5)
The Swords of Babylon (Matt Drake #6)
Blood Vengeance (Matt Drake #7)
Last Man Standing (Matt Drake #8)
The Plagues of Pandora (Matt Drake #9)
The Lost Kingdom (Matt Drake #10)
The Ghost Ships of Arizona (Matt Drake #11)
The Last Bazaar (Matt Drake #12)
The Edge of Armageddon (Matt Drake #13)
The Treasures of Saint Germain (Matt Drake #14)
Inca Kings (Matt Drake #15)
The Four Corners of the Earth (Matt Drake #16)
The Seven Seals of Egypt (Matt Drake #17)
Weapons of the Gods (Matt Drake #18)
The Blood King Legacy (Matt Drake #19)
Devil's Island (Matt Drake #20)
The Fabergé Heist (Matt Drake #21)
Four Sacred Treasures (Matt Drake #22)
The Sea Rats (Matt Drake #23)
Blood King Takedown (Matt Drake #24)
Devil's Junction (Matt Drake #25)
Voodoo soldiers (Matt Drake #26)
The Carnival of Curiosities (Matt Drake #27)

Theatre of War (Matt Drake #28)
Shattered Spear (Matt Drake #29)
Ghost Squadron (Matt Drake #30)
A Cold Day in Hell (Matt Drake #31)
The Winged Dagger (Matt Drake #32)
Two Minutes to Midnight (Matt Drake #33)

The Alicia Myles Series
Aztec Gold (Alicia Myles #1)
Crusader's Gold (Alicia Myles #2)
Caribbean Gold (Alicia Myles #3)
Chasing Gold (Alicia Myles #4)
Galleon's Gold (Alicia Myles #5)

The Torsten Dahl Thriller Series
Stand Your Ground (Dahl Thriller #1)

The Relic Hunters Series
The Relic Hunters (Relic Hunters #1)
The Atlantis Cipher (Relic Hunters #2)
The Amber Secret (Relic Hunters #3)
The Hostage Diamond (Relic Hunters #4)
The Rocks of Albion (Relic Hunters #5)
The Illuminati Sanctum (Relic Hunters #6)
The Illuminati Endgame (Relic Hunters #7)
The Atlantis Heist (Relic Hunters #8)
The City of a Thousand Ghosts (Relic Hunters #9)

All genuine comments are very welcome at:

davidleadbeater2011@hotmail.co.uk

Twitter: @dleadbeater2011

Visit David's website for the latest news and
information:
davidleadbeater.com

Hawaiian Gold

PROLOGUE

Hawaii, 1779

Koa woke that fateful morning with very little on his mind except work. He was a strong, fit, healthy boy and knew his place among the people. He loved the dawn, loved to watch the blood-red sun drift steadily over the horizon. Sometimes, he ventured out early on his own to hide among the trees and watch the splendour unfold, watch as the burning crimson ball chased away the last vestiges of the night to bring its nourishing warmth to the land.

It started out a good day. He joined with his family, his parents and his brothers, working their small plot of land near the coast of the big island of Hawaii. He enjoyed the digging and the fetching and carrying and the brief break they took to eat. When the sun was at its hottest, they took shelter, sitting under the trees and enjoying the stillness. They talked among themselves. Today, their father would meet the chief.

Of course, they had met the chief many times. Sometimes, he worked among them. But, today, their father would be blessed with a great honour. Koa wasn't entirely sure of the significance of it – something to do with their family plot – but it was a privilege, nonetheless. In the afternoon, Koa slipped away from his family and walked the forests for a while

– he loved to walk – and sat for a while by a whispering stream with the sun dappling through the trees all around him, the sounds of the wildlife that teemed between them loud in his ears. Koa stretched out and slept for a short while and, by the time he awakened, the sun wasn't so intense. The first sound he heard was a cry for help.

Koa sat up so quickly his head span. He blinked, wiped his face. *What am I hearing? What is that sound far away?*

It was angry, roaring, faint, but still an assault to the ears. It was the sound of many men fighting.

Koa felt his stomach twist. In his fourteen years, he had been witness to several battles among the natives. He had seen white men come and go, some most recently during the season of Makahiki, the ancient Hawaiian New Year festival. He had seen internal fighting and friends slain and marauders arrive from other islands. It never ended well.

Koa thought about his father, his older brothers. If there was a fight, they would be involved. His stomach clenched even harder. They were all vulnerable to attack; his entire family. Koa rose to his feet.

He carried an axe. He staggered forward, legs like jelly. Images of his friends floated before his eyes and he found it hard to see. He walked into a tree, stepped back, slipped around and started walking faster, heading towards the coast, bypassing his village because he knew the sounds of fighting came from the beach.

It was a journey fraught with tension and fear. Natives didn't have a lot to dread on the island of Hawaii, but they were afraid of their neighbours, warriors from other islands. No chief yet had managed to unite them all, to take Oahu and Maui and Lanai and all the others under a protective wing; there was just too much infighting. Maybe... one day... a worthy chief would arise.

Koa raced through foliage and undergrowth, leaping over fallen branches and twisting between the gnarly trunks of thick trees. The sun beat down hard, making sweat drip from his face. He wondered what their great chief, the inestimable Kalani'opu'u, called the Hawaiian king by some, was doing and what might have gone wrong.

Koa finally broke through the treeline and approached the cliff high above the beach. The sounds of battle were much louder here, screaming and shouting and the unmistakable sharp reports of gunfire. The first thing he saw ahead was the vast, unravelling vista of the ocean, the sparkling expanse bouncing the bright sun back into his eyes. Koa blinked as he ran, trying to blur the image on his retina.

The second thing he saw were the ships.

The same ships, he believed, that had stayed here recently and then departed. They certainly looked the same, although one was missing its foremast. Even then, it occurred to Koa that the ships had returned to make repairs.

But last time, during Makahiki, the natives had tolerated the ships and their sailors. The captain who led them, the man they called Cook, spoke well and brought weapons and gifts with him, and the sailors mostly stayed at sea.

Koa reached the edge of the cliff and looked down. The sight was worse than expected. The whole beach below was a mass of fighters. Koa's eyes widened, his mouth stretched into an O. In the thick of it, there

wasn't a grain of sand to be seen. Nothing but a
sweating mess of struggling men fighting with axes and
spears and swords. Around the peripheries, other men
tried to get involved or fought among themselves. In
the shallows, there were the small boats that the sailors
used to come to shore from the big ships. Uniformed
men were standing in the boats, muskets to their
shoulders, and firing into the crowd of Hawaiian
warriors. There also appeared to be some kind of
restraint. Some soldiers had their muskets reversed
and were using them as clubs. Either that, or they had
run out of gunpowder.

Koa fell to his knees. He could see the dead on both
sides, see the wounded. He could hear them too, their
agonised wails. It was a harsh sight, and it had come on
a beautiful day, out of the blue.

Koa saw many small boats on the beach. The sailors
had arrived in force. Maybe that was part of the reason
Kalani'opu'u had ordered the attack. Koa now saw their
chief in the middle of the battle, surrounded by brawny
men and shouting orders. He carried a large club and
wore a headdress. So far, the battle itself hadn't
reached him.

Koa searched the faces below for his family. It was
so crammed, so violent, down there he could not make
everything out. The sound travelled up the cliff face
like a hard clout to the face, slapping Koa as it roared
past. He saw men trading blows, roaring, forced along
in a crowd of their fellow-warriors. He saw individual
battles, swords against clubs and axes and other
weapons. Men falling to their knees, reaching up to
ward off the next blow only to be felled by it. There was
flailing and vicious punching, people slipping in the
sand, crawling away. Some had reached the shallows

and were up to their ankles or knees, splashing left and right and trying to stay on their feet, thrusting and thumping and assailing each other.

'There you are,' Koa said, spying someone else he knew.

One man stood out from it all. The great mystery man. His name was Kamehameha and, though still young, he was already giving an excellent account of himself. Kamehameha was a bit of a legend around the village – the man was good *mana*. Now, Koa had taken a bit of time to understand *mana*. And understand he had to do, because it was the keystone of the Hawaiian religion. *Mana* was the forceful and prevalent energy of the spirit. The more *mana* you accrued, the more powerful you were considered to be. *Mana* swam around Kamehameha like a tidal current, like a wondrous shoal of fish. Rumours swarmed him. And rumours were nothing without a display of power. Kamehameha gave that today, fighting valiantly away from the major thrust of the battle, taking the invaders down one by one with mighty swings of his axe and club.

But it was then that another figure caught Koa's eye. Captain Cook, the man who called himself a British explorer. Cook was half-fighting, half-gesticulating. He was pointing at a longboat that lay halfway up the beach. Too far to have run aground, but far enough to have been dragged to that position. The sight of it weighed on Koa's heart.

That was it? That was the reason for all this? Several times during the last visit, some of the village upstarts had taken to stealing the British sailors' possessions. The only way the British retrieved their stolen goods was to take some of the Hawaiians hostage. When the goods were returned, so were the Hawaiians. Strangely, it seemed to work out fine for both sides.

At least... last time.

Now, something had changed. The longboat was close to where Chief Kalani'opu'u was standing and where Cook was aiming for. Koa wondered if Cook had come too close to Kalani'opu'u, if the natives thought maybe Cook was trying to kidnap him. Koa could then understand their outrage. You did not lay hands on the chief, the king. It was too much. It could have been a misunderstanding, but now it had escalated beyond repair.

Gunshots rang out from the sea. The British were trying to withdraw, to get their men off the beach and into the waiting boats, but the Hawaiians had surrounded them and were cutting many off, including their leader, Cook. Koa winced as he saw weapons fall harshly and struck out when he saw his fellow men fall to the beach, bleeding heavily. He felt his limbs move involuntarily, felt drawn to the battle, yearned to help defend their homes, but knew he was too young. He had had very little battle training and could not hold his own against grown men. Of course, his brothers, just a few short years ahead of him, would be down there right now, fighting, though Koa couldn't yet see them amid the thousands of natives, townspeople, local men and women. The only people he could properly make out were those at the edge of the beach.

Koa wept inside for those who were dying, even the enemy. He was a sensitive boy and had grown up caring for life in all its wonderful forms, from animals to plants and men and women, good and bad. Koa loved the land, the land of Hawaii, and all the good and amazing things it provided for the people.

But now the beach ran red with blood. The surf was tinged crimson. Everything normally good was tainted. Koa's life had changed in an instant. The anchored ships out there looked hugely intimidating and were filled with fighting men. More longboats were being loosed. Koa could see no end to the battle; it all just seemed to be escalating. He crept as close to the cliff edge as he dared.

Koa felt alone, vulnerable. Everything he knew, his whole life, struggled in uncertain warfare on that beach. A future. Stability. Love. Joy. A home. Family. Koa trembled with uncertainty and berated himself for his weakness.

Cook was close to Kalani'opu'u. The natives all around were fighting viciously. Kalani'opu'u was on the floor, sitting in the sand. Cook reached for him, yelling in his face. Kalani'opu'u shook his head in refusal. Cook tried again. Stentorian cries rang up, even louder than the all-encompassing battle. It looked to Koa as if Cook was trying to take Kalani'opu'u. It was only later he wondered if Cook had been beseeching the man, or trying to help him up.

Whatever it was, the chief was having none if it. Koa saw Kamehameha closing in from the right too, fighting through the fringes and then the heart of the battle. Cook was back to his feet, standing, his sword in one hand. With a dismissive gesture, he struck Kalani'opu'u on the top of his head with the flat of his sword.

And then Cook turned away.

It was then that one of the chief's guards attacked. He flew at Cook with his deadly *leiomano*, his shark-toothed club, smashing him a harsh blow across the back of the head. The captain fell to his knees in the sand. It was then that Kalani'opu'u's other guard brandished a long metal knife, one of the many objects traded by the British during their stay on the Hawaiian islands.

Cook fell face-first into the water, his body convulsing. The chief's guard stepped away. Kalani'opu'u rose to his feet, shouting. The British sailors opened fire once more, but the Hawaiians chased them to the edge of the beach and through the shallows to their longboats. Here, they were fired upon by other sailors and fell to the ground.

Koa knew instinctively that something extremely bad had occurred. Kalani'opu'u was staring, his face expressionless. Even the mysterious, powerful Kamehameha had stopped in his tracks and was now regarding the barely moving body of Captain Cook in the shallows. An emotion that Koa recognised as shock settled over him.

What happens now?

Everything was up in the air, just like Koa's stomach. He was terrified. The leader of the explorers was dying, stabbed by a Hawaiian native. Below, on the beach, the townspeople were incensed. Koa saw that Captain Cook had stopped moving, still face down in the eddying water. The sailors were retreating across the waves, pulling for the longships, but still reloading, pointing their weapons and firing, killing the natives who stood on the beach. Koa thought he could see at least four sailors lying dead besides Captain Cook.

He sighed heavily. The natives swarmed Cook's body. They carried it up out of the shallows and then across the beach. Kalani'opu'u was at their head, directing them. Koa felt unease, but he also felt pride in his people, a deep dignity that they had won the battle and fought the explorers off. Koa rose and ran, trying to reach his people as they climbed the cliff.

They brought the body to the cliff top, in full view of the anchored boats, and there they tore it to pieces. They were enraged, protective of their chief. Koa met up with his parents and his brothers, happy to see them unharmed.

It was another six days before the sailors left in their big ships.

And all the while, the natives watched them and none more than the mystery man, Kamehameha.

CHAPTER ONE

Kalani was lying low in the abandoned old house on the outskirts of Oahu. He was good at lying low. He knew the islands like the back of his hands and had a lot of — well, *low level* — friends scattered across the main ones. Kalani was born in Hawaii. He grew up there, learned to swim and surf and steal there, became a man there.

Why the hell are you hiding?

The internal monologue sprung up now, as it always did. Usually, Kalani had a bit of weed on hand to quell the droning questions, but not today. And, in any case, the answer was pretty damn obvious.

They were after him.

Kalani was a low level crook. He didn't like what he did — carrying and fetching and delivering. He preferred to stay on the fringes of it all, not getting too involved because, seriously, he was embarrassed by what he did. Even the cops didn't bother with him anymore – he wasn't worth their time. Kalani eked out a living as a delivery boy, and so what if he'd skimmed off the tiniest bit on the side? Did it really matter?

Kalani found himself in a strange situation. He had been told by one of his many friends – Kalani was well-liked from Kauai to the Big Island – that one of the criminal organisation's big bosses wanted to talk to him. The information had sent ice water flooding down Kalani's spine. Which big boss, he had asked.

Gouda, he was told.

Kalani had closed his eyes, his entire body now freezing and shaking. Gouda, named after the cheese he loved so much, was the worst asshole of the lot. The chief killer. Gouda enjoyed it. But not just enjoyed. *Gouda sought it out.* He tried repeatedly to get his fellow criminals into trouble, sought out the slightest offence, so that he could justify maltreatment. Now, one might think that, in the criminal world, someone might quickly dispose of such a man, but Gouda had the eyes and ears of the *big* boss, the great Kahuna himself, so Gouda was practically untouchable.

Kalani had stayed away from men like Gouda all his life, giving them no reason to know that he even existed. Kalani preferred to keep it that way. It was why he stayed low level. He didn't even class himself as a criminal, but if he needed to do a few transport jobs to keep himself afloat, then that was what life forced him to do. Kalani didn't like it, but he kept his head down and carried it through, feeling the guilt raise its ugly head afterwards.

How long can you hide out here?

Kalani knew the gang seeking him was good at what they did. They were high level, a black storm-cloud that crept across all of Hawaii. Kalani had found a few tins of food and had brought a bottle of water with him, but beyond that, he had nothing. He was scared. He wasn't a bad person. Why would a man like Gouda be looking for him?

Realistically, of course, the answer was obvious.

Whenever Kalani worked for the gang, his job usually involved transporting sizeable sums of cash from one place to another. Kalani knew this because he always peered into the cloth bags or plastic suitcases they told him to carry. Kalani peered into these bags because... well, because he felt it was his right to extract a couple of the bills for himself. The recipient would never miss fifty dollars, right? And Kalani could certainly use it. Fifty dollars didn't go far these days.

Kalani was sitting on the floor, on a threadbare carpet, looking up at a chipped window sill. He worried that the people who owned this house might return from their vacation early. He worried that a neighbour might come around to check on it. He worried that the same network that had warned him about Gouda and then told him this house was empty might just inform Gouda of the same thing. Being a criminal, even a peripheral one, wasn't easy. Kalani had never been all that good at it.

Of course, his heart wasn't truly in it. That was the real problem. Kalani had fallen into the life and now allowed the life to lead him, *drag* him through various gutters on its way to... where? Where would he end up?

Well, here... in this beaten up old house. His last refuge. Where could he go now to escape a criminal cartel? To escape the dreaded Gouda?

Something glimmered in Kalani's mind. There was an option, a way out. When Kalani wasn't working for the criminal gangs, he was exploring. That was why he knew the islands back to front, why he had so many contacts from shore to shore. He spent his time travelling between them, seeing friends, always on the move. Kalani was flighty and difficult to track down at the best of times. When he resurfaced, it was only because he was short of money. Kalani loved Hawaii, its tradition, its powerful heritage. He liked to go places where the *mana* was strong, where he could stand and feel the spiritual power all around him, filling him, making him feel rich. There were many places across the islands where you could do that. Kalani loved to immerse himself in it. He'd learned that the ancient Hawaiians embraced the language fully because there was no writing in ancient Hawaii. Language was everything. He loved some of the old proverbs and often re-quoted them in his head and out loud to himself. The feel of the words on his tongue quieted the demons in his brain.

Noho me ka hau'oli.

A simple phrase that meant *be happy* but rolled off the tongue like a work of art. Kalani recited it now, feeling instant relief. The sparkling glimmers in his brain grew brighter.

There could be a way out of all this.

It would be difficult, but Kalani was no stranger to hardship. He'd been living hard since his father threw him out seven years ago, when he was fifteen, in a drunken stupor. Kalani had never known his mother. She'd died giving birth to him. Kalani's father seemed to blame him for that – things had never been good between them. Kalani's father used the boy to get his anger out, to ease his frustrations. Kalani had almost welcomed the peace and quiet the street and the land gave him. He found he could exist in the wild as well as anywhere.

He knew the land, knew its ways, its beauty and its dangers. One reason the cops had given up on him was that Kalani could vanish for weeks on end, living off the bounty that was Oahu and Maui and Molokai.

But it wasn't any of those three that had provided big time. It was a different island. Kalani had been trying to decide what to do about it for weeks. At first, he'd put the find out of his mind, tried to live with it. But that would never work. The find was too significant; it was life changing, world changing, history changing. Kalani knew he couldn't let it lie. The massive implications ate at him.

He was still deciding what to do when the Gouda information reached him.

Now... what? The gang had eyes and ears on every island except Nihau, the forbidden isle. And, clearly, Kalani couldn't go there. Nobody was allowed there. But if anyone could slip through the surveillance, then it was Kalani.

But sitting here right now, unobserved, felt good.

Here, nobody could grab him, catch him, take him to Gouda. Here... he was safe.

Wasn't he?

Kalani wasn't sure what to believe. Yes, the bad guys could find him. He wasn't entirely off the radar. Maybe he should fix that.

Again, his mind went back to the *find*. It was incredibly significant. He couldn't just let it be. Kalani thought better with a reefer between his lips, but right now, that was an impossible dream. He stretched out, decided he shouldn't relax too much, and sat upright again, peering over the windowsill into the overgrown front garden.

The road beyond was empty. No sign of Gouda and his goons rolling up.

Kalani wondered how impossibly rich he might become. The find was astronomical. Of course, the find was more for the people of Hawaii than anything else, but with that kind of fame Kalani knew the money was sure to follow. He would be famous the world over, famous and rich, and... easier to find?

Gouda was a problem. To be fair, it was a problem Kalani had created for himself, just as life was improving. Why was it that when one half of your life started to improve dramatically, the other took a sharp swan dive into the crapper? Why was that? Kalani thought it had something to do with *mana*, with how much life-force you had accumulated.

'So what next?' he asked himself.

He said, *'A'ohe pu'u ki'eki'e ke ho'a'ho 'ia e pi'i.'*

No cliff is so tall it cannot be climbed.

Peace washed over him. The proverb had a deep meaning. He kept it close to his heart. He let the word *Kamehameha* wash through his brain. The single word electrified him. They'd been searching for centuries for the great one. The greatest one of all. The spiritual king of all the islands.

Kalani swallowed drily. He shifted, unable to stay still. It was then, *right then,* as he allowed himself an indulgent moment of joy, that he heard the door slamming outside the house. He blinked, rose, lifted his eyes above the windowsill.

He gawped.

They were here. He counted eight of them. They wore cut-off t-shirts and leather jackets and they were stalking angrily towards the house. Kalani saw knives and guns in their hands; they weren't bothered who might see them. He rose as fast as an electrified meerkat and bolted. Ran for the back door. He'd already scouted a way out of here.

Obviously.

The trouble was, the bad guys were already at the back door. They'd come in force. The first thing Kalani saw as he dashed through the kitchen was Gouda's eyes meeting his through the door's window pane.

Gouda smiled.

And Kalani heard the awful, grating voice.

'I want to have a word with you.'

CHAPTER TWO

They shoved Kalani roughly into the back of a car, the compartment lid closed even as he tried to protest his innocence. The small, compact area smelt of oil and, faintly, of bleach. Kalani wondered why they would use bleach in the rear of a car. The vehicle started up and then drove none too gently for about an hour, first quickly along country roads that twisted and turned and then slowly through stop-start traffic. Kalani got the feeling he was being driven to the gang's HQ just outside Honolulu.

He searched the interior for an escape latch, any kind of way out, but there was nothing. The gang had removed everything he might use. Kalani had no option but to lie there and worry about what would happen next.

He heard nothing except the rumble of the road and the occasional sound drifting in from the outside. The sound of a siren. Shouting from people on the streets. The blaring of car horns and the grumble of an engine. Kalani sweated, and it wasn't just the rising temperature. Truth be told, he didn't want the ride to end.

All too soon, it did. The car jerked to a stop, doors cracked open. Kalani heard footsteps and then the lid flew open and his eyes were stung with light. Hands reached down, grabbed him, and hauled him out.

Kalani stood, swaying on the concrete, slightly unsteady. His eyes grew accustomed to the light as he looked around.

Yes, this was the gang's HQ all right.

Kalani breathed deeply, trying not to show how scared he was. The men gathered around him were simple thugs, all brawn and nothing up top. They waited in place for Gouda to give them their orders.

Soon enough, Gouda slithered out of the front seat of another car, looked over at Kalani and gave him a grin. Kalani wasn't impressed. Gouda's grin was bristling with evil. The guy looked happy. Kalani knew why.

They led Kalani quickly off the street, took him through the front doors of an office and then through the working bays of a garage. Kalani saw several cars up on ramps getting work done to their exhausts or undersides. He saw mechanics leaning into engines, spanners and mole wrenches in their free hands. Nobody looked up as he was led through.

Up a set of rear stairs, onto the first floor now, through a box room and then along a narrow corridor. It was dark down here, and getting quieter, the only sounds being the steps of the men pushing him along. Kalani felt isolated, alone, at the mercy of his captors. He could barely believe this was happening to him.

Someone had sold him out. Someone had informed Gouda that he was staying at the house. There were low level criminals like Kalani, and then there were the real bottom dwellers. The trash that would sell you out their friends and family for a small packet of snow, the human garbage that lived in the sewer.

Someone pushed Kalani bodily through a wooden door, striking his head on the panels. He fell into a square room with one window. Taking a quick glance through it, Kalani saw landmarks and knew instantly where he was. He also knew from his observations on the way up here that there was a balcony outside the window and a parking area directly below. He doubted the information would do him any good.

A lone chair sat in the middle of the room. They directed Kalani to sit down on it.

He did as he was told, still trying not to reveal any sign of fear.

'Why am I here?' he asked one goon, a face he recognised.

'Yo, brah, you *lolo*. You be found out.'

Kalani knew the slang, the pidgin Hawaiian. He was being called crazy, stupid. *You be found out*. Shit, that didn't sound good. He wondered if there was anything he could say to help his case. He wondered how far Gouda would go.

The problem was... Gouda was a mental case. As Kalani already knew, Gouda enjoyed this kind of thing.

Kalani had never felt so alone in his life. Yes, he was raised without a proper Ohana, a family. Ohana was the centre of traditional life; it was a mainstay that shouldn't be overlooked. But now... now he was surrounded by people who wanted to kill him because they thought he'd done wrong, that he'd betrayed them.

Some believed the criminal gang itself was Ohana. Kalani didn't accept that. Nothing that dwelt in evil could be Ohana. He'd learned that from his dad.

Right then, Gouda walked into the room.

Kalani stared at the man. Gouda was tall, wore expensive clothes, and was often draped in gold jewellery. His neck swam with gold, as did his arms, and his teeth had gold fillings. His fingers bristled with golden rings which, currently, he was slowly twisting off.

Gouda approached Kalani.

'Hey, brah, nice of you to join us.'

Gouda's voice was a whispery rush, all threat and intimidation. He couldn't help it. That was just the way he spoke. But it didn't exactly do him any harm, either.

'I didn't have a lot of choice,' Kalani said softly.

'There are two ways we can do this,' Gouda said. 'The simple way, or the Gouda way. You choose.'

Kalani bit his lip, not entirely sure what Gouda was saying. He assumed the simple way was to tell the truth and the Gouda way simmered in violence. But you never could be too sure with Gouda.

'Let's try the simple way,' he said.

And Gouda walked up to him, clenched his hand into a fist and delivered a blow to Kalani's right cheek. The blow snapped Kalani's head back. The men gathered around the room laughed.

'Simple it is,' Gouda said. He waited for Kalani to settle once more and then delivered a blow to his left cheek. Kalani closed his eyes from the pain and brought a hand up to rub his jaw.

'It feels more like the Gouda way,' Kalani said.

'Is that you being smart? I wouldn't advise it. Being smart in here will get you a knife in the ribs. And that'd just be the start.'

Kalani held up both hands. 'Sorry.'

Gouda used the movement to take a low shot at Kalani's belly. The blow smashed all the breath out of him and threw his head forward. It made Kalani's insides twist as though he was going to throw up.

'Confess,' Gouda said.

'To what?' Kalani gritted his teeth. If he confessed, they would kill him.

'We already know what you did.'

'I'm nothing. A low level courier. I couldn't possibly hurt... the organisation. What did I do?'

Gouda studied him, narrow-eyed for a minute. Then he stepped back and motioned to the goons who were standing around.

'Search him.'

They were searching for wires, Kalani knew. Wires that would lead to a microphone and a few local police, or a fed's, ears. They ripped his t-shirt all the way up and then checked inside his trousers, his pants. It was an indignity.

'I'm not working against you,' he said when it was all over.

'You're a petty thief, Kalani,' Gouda said. 'A worthless shit-eating asshole who doesn't know a good thing when it knocks at his front door. You are garbage to me, something I might scrape off the bottom of my shoe.'

Kalani was tempted to say, *You know where the door is,'* but kept his mouth shut.

'You've been skimming,' now Gouda leaned forward as he got into the meat of it. 'A few dollars here, a few there. You thought we would never notice. But... Kalani... we're not as stupid as you. We're *omni-fucking-potent.'*

Kalani had had plenty of time to come up with something, anything that might prolong his life. But right now, he couldn't think of anything. He looked from Gouda to the other thugs in the room, hoping for some help, some consideration, even a little remorse maybe.

'He's too scared to speak,' one man guffawed. 'Slit his throat, Gouda.'

So much for compassion.

Kalani knew he had to say something and time was running out. He swallowed and then spoke. 'Listen,' he said. 'It's not me. Someone else is ripping you guys off. Please believe me, brah. Why would I do this? I'm low level. Lowest level. Not even worthy of your attention. And I know I have it good here. A job every now and again keeps the dollars flowing in. Why would I risk that?'

Gouda raised an eyebrow, as if considering the question. Then he reached behind him, into his waistband, and brought out a knife. He held it up to catch the light that was beaming in through the room's only window.

'Time to do it the Gouda way.'

'You don't need to do that, brah.'

'Oh, I know. But it's more fun this way.'

Gouda was an evil son of a bitch. He laid the blade flat against Kalani's cheek and let it slide down the soft skin. He aimed the point at Kalani's eyebrow and brought it closer and closer until Kalani was leaning back with the chair on two legs. Next, he levelled the blade at Kalani's balls and pressed hard. Kalani's trousers split.

'Please,' he said.

'Where to start?' Gouda grinned from ear to ear.

'How about with that guy over there?' Kalani nodded at a guy bigger than the Hulk.

'Oh, funny right until the end, I see. Well, brah, you're gonna need some of that humour to get you through the next hour or two.'

Hour or two?

Kalani closed his eyes, no longer able to hide the fear. It should never have come this far. He was stupid; he was a fool; he was everything they thought he was.

'Why would you steal from us?' Gouda said, as if reading his mind.

'Please don't kill me.'

'And prevent Gouda from having his fun?' one goon laughed. 'That'll never happen, kid.'

'I'm gonna slice you up, brah,' Gouda breathed in his face, smelling of onions and garlic. 'I'm gonna gag you and make it last. See you squirm and bleed. I wanna see your *bones*, do you understand? I wanna see every bone through ripped open flesh. I wanna carve my name on those bones. And then maybe... maybe... I'll rip your throat out with my teeth. After that, we'll make sure they find the body to deter others who might have the same stupid ideas.'

Kalani shivered. Otherwise, he couldn't move. He saw the knife move out of sight, felt it rest against his shin. Gouda was ready to start. Kalani had no way out. He pulled back as far as he could. There was nowhere else to go.

He felt the prick of the knife against this skin.

'Wait!' he cried. 'Wait! I have something for you!'

Gouda looked up at him and frowned.

'A treasure! Worth millions. Maybe billions.'

Gouda rose to his feet and leaned forward. 'What treasure?'

'*Kamehameha!*'

Gouda blinked rapidly. Then his face screwed up. 'What the fuck are you talking about?'

'The greatest Hawaiian mystery,' Kalani told him. 'I know where King Kamehameha is buried.'

CHAPTER THREE

It amazed Kalani when Gouda took a step back.

'You believe me?'

Gouda actually looked bewildered. Kalani hadn't taken him for a traditional Hawaiian, but he had banked on the man's greed.

'Why should I believe you?'

Kalani had expected this question. 'I can't prove it here,' he said. 'We have to make some kind of deal.'

'Easily done,' Gouda said. 'Tell me where he is right now or I'll slit your throat.'

Kalani shook his head. 'That's not gonna work for me.'

'Last chance,' Gouda levelled the knife again, this time at Kalani's throat.

'Listen to me. I can't go with you. If I do, once you've found the bones, you're just going to kill me. Right there and then. Probably dump me alongside Kamehameha.'

'You want us to take the word of a liar and a thief?'

'Well... yeah.'

'I should just kill you now.'

'But you can't, can you? Because you think I'm telling the truth. And I am. I know exactly where King Kamehameha is buried and I could lead you right to his tomb.'

'Have you seen the treasure?'

'The gold and jewels that he was buried with? Oh, yes. It's piled up all around him.'

Gouda narrowed his eyes. 'Then why didn't you bring any with you?'

'Out of the cave? Oh, that would be sacrilege. Not just that, but imagine if centuries old coins started appearing across the islands. Even worse, imagine trying to trade them for cold cash. Warning signals would start popping off everywhere. No, this needs to be done properly, my friend.'

'Properly?'

'No half-assed criminal enterprise is gonna get away with finding the bones of Kamehameha and claiming a reward. Don't forget, those bones and what comes with them belong to the state of Hawaii. They may offer you a percentage of the total value as a finder's fee. *May.*'

'Wait,' Gouda tapped Kalani on the head with the flat of his knife. 'Half-assed?'

Kalani made a rueful face. 'Yeah, umm, that was just an example.'

'What did you have in mind?'

'Your best way of taking all the value for yourself is to go find a private collector. Someone with more money than sense, someone who would take Kamehameha's remains and lock them away in a private vault. That kind of person.'

Gouda regarded him evenly. 'You've put some thought into this.'

Truth be told, Kalani had thought about little else these past few weeks. Of course, he'd never resort to calling a private collector. Kamehameha belonged to the people of Hawaii. Kalani's thought processes revolved more around trying to decide who he should approach, someone who couldn't be corrupted. Because, once the secret got out...

It didn't bear thinking about. This was the find of the century. No, for Hawaii, it was the greatest find in all of history. Once they heard about it, despicable men and women would be looking to make a few bucks; they'd be oozing up through the floorboards, creeping out of the walls; they'd be circling the treasure like a pack of carrion, trying to pick off morsels. Kalani wanted to negate their influence as far as he could.

And that meant going to the right people in the first place.

None of whom were in this room.

Gouda was watching him carefully. 'First,' he said. 'We have to find out if you're telling the truth.'

Kalani shrugged. 'I understand that.'

'You know what happens if you're not?'

'I've heard all the threats. Knives. Blood. Bone. Carving. Murder.'

'That would be the least of it.'

Kalani wondered what the hell else they could do to him, but it probably wasn't a good idea to ask. He was sure Gouda would come up with something imaginative. He saw the uncertainty in Gouda's eyes and ladled heaps of extra temptation onto his proposition.

'Think about it. If you're Hawaiian, you know about Kamehameha. You know the story, all the stories. There isn't a more important ruler in the world. What wouldn't you do to find his remains?'

'Some Hawaiians believe the King should forever rest in peace,' one of the larger goons spoke up.

'I can respect that.' Kalani bowed his head. 'I understand it. But that's not the issue here.'

He knew Gouda was on the hook. He could tell Gouda was already trying to figure out what to tell the boss. Gouda still held the knife, but he aimed the point at the floor. It occurred to Kalani then that he did not know who the boss was.

'You gonna report this?' he asked. 'If you want to take it further. I mean...'

It came out more garbled than he wanted. Yes, he was still scared. Was there a proverb for this situation? *Probably,* he thought. But right now, it wouldn't come to mind.

'Kamehameha,' Gouda said. 'The King. And you believe you've found his tomb,' he laughed. 'Why should I believe you?'

Kalani sensed trouble. 'Why would I lie? I'm just prolonging the inevitable if I'm lying.' It was entirely possible that Gouda had decided not to accept Kalani's words. That he didn't want to get into what was clearly going to be a laborious process.

'Your boss,' he said. 'Would surely want to know about this.'

Gouda waved the knife back and forth. At that moment, two of the goons were called out of the room, which left two more and Gouda. The two who remained were stationed by the door. Kalani sent a hooded glance towards the window.

When it came to a choice of die or die trying to escape, Kalani was all for the latter. Gouda clearly wasn't convinced. Even if the bad guys took him at his word, Kalani would be killed off as soon as he led them to the treasure. Of that, he had no doubt. He was just prolonging the inevitable.

Live another day.

It wasn't a bad proverb to exist by. It worked for some more than others, he guessed, but it would do.

Kalani tried once more. 'Hey, brah, do you wanna take it to your boss?'

Gouda fixed a hard glare on him. 'The bosses want you dead,' he said. 'More than dead, actually. Either way, you're going in the ground, *brah.*'

'Wow, that's some incredible incentive. And you have bosses? I never knew.'

'Oh, I got three of 'em,' Gouda shook his head as if exasperated. 'You try attending a board meeting with Lynskey and two other la—' Gouda stopped himself, realising that his mouth had been running away with itself.

'Go on,' Kalani said, but inside he was reeling. *Lynskey?* He knew the name Lynskey all too well, and he couldn't believe what he was hearing.

Gouda pulled away, turned to the guards by the door, and waved the knife at them. 'Bring me the tools.'

Tools?

Kalani didn't like the sound of that. He was hyper aware that it was fight-or-flight time. And surprise, yes *surprise,* would win the day.

Kalani surged out of his seat and took a swipe at Gouda. His right arm collided with the man's left, hitting at the wrist and knocking the knife out of his hand. Gouda's eyes flew wide open, and he blinked even as Kalani lifted a knee and kicked him hard in the groin.

Gouda groaned and sank to his knees.

Kalani saw about six seconds of opportunity. The goons at the door were just staring, their brains not yet fully registering that Kalani was trying to escape. Kalani had carved out a short timeframe. He could only pray for the best now.

He ran past the fallen Gouda as fast as he could, straight at the window. He leapt high when he got close, tucked his arms and legs in, and hit it hard. In his mind was the terrifying image of him just bouncing back off the glass, bouncing back into the room and being dragged upright by the laughing goons.

But when Kalani struck the glass, it shattered all around him. He flew through the pane, broken glass showering everywhere, and launched himself out into midair. Now, he was still one storey up.

He fell. No doubt something would break and he'd be unable to make his escape. But Kalani had gambled. He knew the window overlooked a car park. He gambled that some kind of vehicle was parked underneath him.

And lady luck shined her magic. There was a large transit van. Kalani hit the top of it; the breath rushed out of him. He'd crumpled the metal, but the roof had arrested his fall and saved him. Kalani groaned. Nothing was broken. Speed was everything now. He unfurled his body, still groaning, and jumped down off the roof of the van to the concrete below. He rolled. He stood up.

Looked back up at the window he'd just escaped from.

Gouda was staring out of it, glaring down at him with murder in his eyes.

It was time to run.

CHAPTER FOUR

Alicia Myles didn't like turbulence. When the plane started shuddering and skipping around, she gripped her seat's armrests tightly and held on. She stared straight ahead, running through an old rock song in her mind, trying to take her mind off the juddering, the jerking, and the way the damn metal tube wanted to surf its way through the sky.

Speaking of surf, Alicia tried to remember how long it was since she'd visited Hawaii. Not that long, to be fair. They were here just a few short months ago. Then, a holiday had turned into a fraught chase, but that had been with her other team.

She wondered what Michael Crouch's Gold team had in store for her.

The call had come late one night as they were about to leave London. Yes, they'd prevented a nuclear bomb from exploding at the last minute. Why was it always the last minute? *Correction,* she thought. This time it had been the last *second.*

But the job was done. They were on their way back to Washington, DC. Then the phone had rung. Alicia scooped it up and glared at the screen.

'Shit, it's Michael,' she'd said to her boyfriend, Matt Drake.

'What does he want?'

'Me, I'm assuming. Why else would he be calling?'

Drake had shaken his head. 'Just answer it, love.'

She'd done that. Crouch and the rest of the Gold team needed her help in Hawaii. Alicia had taken about eight seconds to make her mind up.

'I can't leave them in the lurch.'

So now here she was, approaching Hawaii after a long seventeen hour flight in which she'd watched three movies, eaten several helpings of plane food, listened to the guy next to her sing along to fourteen Ava Max songs, and caught about an hour of fitful shuteye. She wasn't complaining. Of course, the turbulence could have gone and fucked off for the entire journey instead of most of it. But really, she wasn't complaining.

The Hawaiian Airlines flight started descending. Alicia was in the middle of a row, so couldn't see the sparkling blue Pacific or the island of Oahu as they flew lower and lower. She held on tight as the plane bumped down and then squealed across the tarmac, then waited for the plane to stop before rising and grabbing her carry on. All she had was carry-on, so, when everyone else headed for the conveyor belts, Alicia breezed right past them and into the terminal proper, where she looked for a taxi sign.

Eight minutes after that, she was heading for Honolulu at breakneck speed.

She'd already texted Crouch. It was 5.30 a.m. in this part of the world, and her boss had texted back to tell her to meet them for breakfast. So it was Denny's on Lewers Street, in the Imperial Hawaiian resort that was open twenty-four hours. Alicia was already looking forward to the endless coffees and the Bourbon Chicken Bowl with blueberry pancakes and maple syrup on the side. She sat back in the car as the driver took her speedily through the traffic towards the high rises.

A little over forty minutes later, she arrived, head swimming with motion sickness, at her destination, paid the taxi driver and paused before the Imperial Hawaiian. She stood for a moment, breathing deeply, focusing. At this time of the morning, Waikiki was mostly tourist free and quiet. She liked the calm, savoured it.

When she walked into Denny's, all that would end.

Alicia thought about her life. She leapt from one lethal chase to another, her feet barely touching the ground. She lived a wild life where nothing was set in stone, not even her own opinions. But that was better than she'd had it in a long time. It was better than ever. Alicia didn't know where she'd end up, but she sure knew where she'd been.

She entered the hotel and found the restaurant. There were three people seated at a table inside, and Alicia knew every one of them.

Caitlyn Nash was an introvert, forever stuck in a place where her father had caused the death of her mother through abuse, who tried to remain in touch with the real world as best she could whilst dealing with her issues. Caitlyn always looked a bit frazzled, but was good-hearted and ready to help.

Rob Russo was an experienced ex-soldier, a behemoth of a man who'd seen blood and death and incredible rage in wars all around the world and kept it all hidden inside. Bad, good, indifferent, he never talked about it. But there were times when Russo became a berserker, unable to quell the rage inside. He and Alicia had a kind of love-hate relationship, something bordering on mutual respect, so long as they remained at arm's length.

Michael Crouch had once run a secretive and highly skilled offshoot of the SAS called the Ninth Division. He had outstanding contacts all over the world and was well known as a sentimentalist. He'd quit the army years ago, tootled around a bit, and then gone on to run a successful treasure-hunting team.

Alicia approached the table. All three rose to their feet, Michael coming out to hug her. Alicia eyed the others as she took a seat.

'Missed me?' she asked.

'So much!' Caitlyn said.

'Like a wasp on my bollocks,' Russo growled.

'You know we have,' Crouch said, and handed her a menu.

Alicia said, 'Guess I've missed you too. Even you, Robster.'

'Thanks for coming,' Crouch said.

'It better be fucking good,' Alicia grumbled as she scanned the menu. 'Seventeen hours from London, from my boyfriend, and then the taxi drive from hell.'

'You have a boyfriend?' Russo asked. 'How many legs does he have?'

Alicia flipped him off. She didn't expect Crouch to explain himself right away, which was just as well because he didn't. First, they ordered their food and sat back as a server filled their mugs with fresh coffee. Alicia watched the other three as she settled in.

'How long have you been here?' she asked.

'Just a couple of days,' Crouch said. 'We had to verify everything before calling you and moving forward. Alicia... I have to say... this is pretty big.'

'Now those are words I do like to hear,' she said with a grin at Russo.

The big man only shook his head at her. Alicia sipped her coffee and glanced around the restaurant. Pictures of Hawaii festooned the walls. There were palm trees standing alone, bent at an angle, and marching down one of Waikiki's major shopping streets. There was the great crater of Diamond Head in contrast to the high-rise buildings of downtown Honolulu. Alicia saw the golden stretch of Waikiki Beach, the historic landmark that was the Aloha Tower, once a lighthouse. She saw a luau scene, complete with fire and dancers and musicians. Just looking at the walls made Alicia think of the beauty of Hawaii and all the natural splendour offered by the islands.

'It's beautiful, isn't it?' Crouch followed her eyes. 'Well, we have something that harks back into all that tradition, into Hawaii's rich past.'

Alicia was ready to hear it and looked at him. 'I've come a long way to hear this, Michael.'

Caitlyn leaned forward enthusiastically. 'We're in the realm of kings and dynasties and important history here. It's more than treasure.'

Alicia smiled at the historian. 'I'm listening.'

'Have you ever heard of Kamehameha?'

'Yeah, vaguely. Wasn't he a Hawaiian king? I believe there are statues of him all over the place.'

'He was one of the most prominent figures of Hawaiian history,' Caitlyn said. 'A king who united and ruled all the islands. The first person to do that. He was born into a royal family in North Kohala and, because of ongoing wars at the time, was taken away from the area, hidden after his birth. He returned at the age of five and received special training from his uncle. This

34

training was extensive, involving warfare, history, navigation, and anything else that would help him become a district chief. He became a superb warrior, described as tall, strong and fearless. There is even a story that once, he even boarded Captain Cook's vessel, the Discovery. Anyway, through civil war and jockeying for power, Kamehameha grew from a chief to the man who would unite Hawaii. And as you say, there are statues of him everywhere from here in Waikiki to Washington, DC.'

'He sounds like he was a great man,' Alicia said.

'Oh, he was,' Crouch said. 'With his armies, he invaded Oahu, Maui, Molokai and more. He traded with countless foreign ships, made allies everywhere. He built economies and learned warfare from the foreigners. He built an armada of war canoes armed with cannons and taught his highly capable warriors how to use muskets. There is nothing small about Kamehameha. He was the very large, very real deal.'

'Okay, I'm getting that he was important and valuable to Hawaii,' Alicia said. 'But why are you telling me all this?'

'Well, when Kamehameha was satisfied with his conquests, he made the journey to Kailua-Kona where he spent seven years in retirement. His years in power had been due to political alignments and conspiracies, to invasion and to civil war. But the islands were now united, as one, no longer a scarred land of warring tribes. The man died in May 1819, having secured the future of his people.'

Alicia drank half her coffee and then waited as the server brought their meals. Soon, they were all tucking into the fare and said nothing for a while. Alicia watched the light outside the far window grow brighter and brighter as the sunrise ignited the morning and climbed the skies. Inside, the restaurant was dimly lit, its yellow lampshades giving off a dull reflective glow.

Alicia waved her fork at Crouch. 'I'm guessing all this has to do with Kamehameha.'

'Very astute of you. Well, as you can imagine, Kamehameha is held in high regard around these parts, as high as any western deity you can imagine. So let me tell you this. After he died, Kamehameha was subject to all the usual Hawaiian rituals, and then he was buried.'

'In secret,' Caitlyn said.

Alicia looked up from her food. 'In secret?'

'Yes,' Crouch went on. 'To this day, despite many attempts, the body of King Kamehameha has never been found. Not a crypt. Not a tomb. Nothing.'

'Obviously, he was hidden for a reason.' Alicia said.

'At his own request. Kamehameha was one of the greatest tacticians to ever live. He planned for his own funeral and burial.'

Alicia blinked. 'And it's not like Hawaii's exactly that big.'

'But it has a hell of a lot of islands,' Caitlyn said. 'And such a diverse range of conditions, from the largest active volcano in the world to rainforests to tropical ecoregions to wide-ranging climates. You can walk atop a mountain above the clouds in Maui, and then walk along Waikiki Beach alongside the blue Pacific ocean on Oahu. The Big Island itself, a relatively small area, hosts four out of five of the known climate groups, that's tropical, arid, temperate and polar.'

'So you're saying the only way to find Kamehameha's tomb is by pure luck?' Alicia said.

'You might say that,' Crouch said with a grin.

Alicia stopped eating. 'What have you found?' she asked.

CHAPTER FIVE

Michael Crouch took a moment to savour his coffee before replying. There was usually no coming between Crouch and his coffee, especially on a morning.

'Not *what*,' he said. '*Who?*'

Alicia finished her meal and pushed the plate away. 'Who?'

'An old friend of mine,' Crouch said. 'A man named Tom Pierce. He's a private detective, living near Waikiki.'

Alicia narrowed her eyes. 'A private detective in Hawaii? Are you kidding me?'

'I know what you're thinking. *Magnum*. Am I right?'

'I was thinking more *Tom Selleck* back in the day.'

'Get your head out of the gutter,' Russo growled.

'I can't help it,' Alicia returned. 'The gutter is where I belong.'

Russo nodded his agreement.

'Anyway, Pierce contacted me a few days ago with an amazing story. We've kept in touch through the years, so he knows about my interests and that we have a team. We—'

'We do?' Alicia said with a brief grin. 'I mean, what do you guys do when I'm off saving the world with Drake's team?'

'What the hell do you think we do?' Russo asked.

'Oh, I don't know. Drink tea? Platt each other's hair? Especially you, Robster. You have the look of a wonderful hairdresser.'

Russo didn't respond, didn't even look at her.

Crouch answered. 'We recently found an old crown in eastern Europe. It was—'

'Who's this guy?' Alicia interrupted.

A man was approaching their table. Alicia had seen him enter through the far door and make a beeline for them. Already, she was half-rising to her feet, knife in hand, prepared for anything. In her job, you had to be. The margins between life and death – and surprise attack – were minute.

'Stand down,' Crouch said. 'That's Pierce.'

'The PI?'

'Yes, I asked him to meet us here.'

Alicia stayed on her feet to greet him. Pierce was about average height, wide and well-muscled. He moved like a soldier to Alicia's trained eye, moved like she did, like everyone she knew did. His eyes rested on her warily as he approached the table.

'Michael,' he said.

Crouch rose to greet him and then introduced everyone. Pierce sat down, rubbed the bristle on his chin, and nodded at Alicia.

'I've heard a lot about you.'

Alicia looked surprised but couldn't stop herself from nodding back at the entrance doors. 'I was expecting a red Ferrari to be parked outside.'

Pierce bit his lip. 'Yeah, I get that a lot from foreigners.'

Alicia blinked. 'I'm not sure I enjoy being called a foreigner,' she said.

'If you're not Hawaiian, you're a foreigner,' Pierce assured her. 'If you're American from the mainland, you're a foreigner. And you guy, especially, are *haole's*.'

'I'm not sure I enjoy being called a *howlee* either,' Alicia said.

'Get used to it,' Pierce said.

Crouch waved to be heard. 'Listen,' he said. 'I called Tom here to meet us so that he could explain to us as a group exactly what he told me. I think you all should hear it from the horse's mouth.'

Alicia signalled for a refill of her coffee and they waited until the server had left.

'All right,' Pierce finally said. 'As you know, I'm a PI. Make a pretty steady living on Oahu, occasionally have to head over to Maui or Kauai or even the Big Island if I need to. Yeah, I know it's a cliché, but I'm an ex-cop and ex-military. Learned everything I know from the army and HPD. Like Michael here, I have a raft of contacts, only mine are spread all over Hawaii. Every island. Every city, town, village, you name it.'

'You're well connected,' Russo said. 'We get it.'

'Of course. Well, one of my connections, a young guy called Kalani, works inside a criminal outfit. He's an informant of sorts, though the outfit is pretty tight and hard to infiltrate. Kalani keeps his butt firmly on the outside of the gang. A wise move. He doesn't wanna get sucked in to that world and just fetches and carries to earn a few bucks here and there. Kalani's ones of those odd ones – not really a criminal, but exists in that world.'

'Kalani sounds unfortunate.' Crouch said. 'Does he have to work in that world?'

'Nothing else for him,' Pierce said. 'Economy's not what it used to be. He gets by. Anyway, like me, Kalani is pretty well known across the islands. Known as a good guy. Like you say 'unfortunate', but good. People like Kalani.'

'Has he gotten himself into something bad?' Caitlyn asked.

'Kalani has gone missing,' Pierce said. 'But it's what he said before he went missing that concerns us.'

Alicia leaned forward. 'And what was that?'

'To be clear, I have another informer in the same gang. They heard what Kalani told a man called Gouda. Now, it seems the idiot was skimming a little off the top whenever he delivered some cash. Just a little, so little he didn't think anyone would notice. But these gangs didn't get to where they were today by being stupid. They expect people to steal, and they're always on the lookout for it. Anyway, Kalani got found out. They took him to their HQ.'

'To kill him?' Caitlyn asked quietly.

Pierce shrugged. 'I guess that was the plan. But my informer tells me that, as they worked on Kalani, as they interrogated him and worked their way up to whatever it was they were going to do, he came out with some crazy story. Screamed out that he knew exactly where Kamehameha was buried, that he could lead them to his tomb. Told them it would be the find of the century. Now...' Pierce looked from face to face. 'I'm assuming you all know who Kamehameha is?'

Alicia nodded. 'We got the lowdown already.'

'Good. So, as you can imagine, the goons were in shock. They're all native Hawaiians. They know what such a find would mean to the world but, mostly, to Hawaii. Even criminals aren't immune to their ancestry. My informant tells me that Kalani then made a break for it.'

'He escaped?' Alicia was surprised.

'He kicked out, ran for the window and jumped through. Remember, they were on the first floor. Kalani made it outside in one piece and ran for it. Escaped and evaded them and is now on the run with some incredibly important information.'

Alicia frowned. 'But it was all bullshit, surely. He fed them what they wanted to hear to cause a distraction.'

'That's not how my informant sees it,' Pierce said. 'And not how I see it. When he revealed his information, it was looking very bad for Kalani. He didn't know how they would react. My informant tells me he was wholly genuine and, knowing Kalani like I do, I believe he was telling the truth.'

'That he found Kamehameha's tomb?' Crouch said, playing Devil's Advocate since he'd heard all this already. 'Can you be sure?'

'Consider that it's also a strange and tall tale to come out with just off the cuff. He had to know they probably wouldn't believe such a wild story. Why try it in the first place if it wasn't true?'

Alicia had to admit that Pierce had a point. There were other, more believable stories that Kalani could have come up with. 'How could he have found the tomb in the first place?' she asked.

'As I explained, Kalani is well travelled. He knows these islands like the back of his hand. Knows the people, the natives. Everyone likes him, and that's because he makes the rounds regularly. He's lived in the wilds too, the hills and the forests, some of the least accessible ones. He goes everywhere, explores everything. It's not that much of a stretch to believe that, on one of his travels, he found something.'

'But why not shout about it?' Russo said.

'Good question. I don't know why he didn't take it to
the authorities. Maybe because he's in that grey area
with them. Maybe he doesn't trust them. Or maybe it's
a recent find.'

'Maybe he's been struggling with it for a while,'
Alicia offered. 'I know how a secret can churn you up.'

Alicia was straight forward and headstrong, but
she'd had her fair share of problems. More than her
fair share, starting at home when she was young. It was
why she'd joined the army in the first place.

'And you want us to help you find Kamehameha?'
Caitlyn asked.

'Kalani,' Pierce said. 'And by association,
Kamehameha. There could be no greater find in
Hawaii's lifetime.'

'Where do we start?' Alicia asked.

CHAPTER SIX

The server brought them more coffee. Alicia had drank so much caffeine her fingers were starting to tap involuntarily on the table and her right eye felt like it wanted to twitch. Still, she took another mug.

'Tell us what you know about this gang,' Crouch said. 'It sounds like they might be quite dangerous.'

Pierce nodded. 'Well organised. Mysterious. Nobody knows who leads the organisation, though it's said to be three men. They rule their patch with an iron hand, don't step on bigger toes, and seem well-drilled, ruthless and dominant. A few years ago, nobody had ever heard of them. Now, they're prevalent. Growing.'

'What do they call themselves?' Alicia recalled her recent escapades in Hawaii as part of Drake's team, where a gang had been involved.

'The 42K,' Pierce said and shrugged. 'I do not know why.'

'The cops can't touch them?'

'They try. Three times the 42K have sued the city for wrongful accusations and won. Cops are warier now; they want to keep their jobs.'

'You do well to have informants in their group?' Russo said, his comment actually an important question that Pierce recognised.

'I'm a likeable kind of guy.' Peirce said shortly.

44

'So you keep saying,' Alicia said. 'But Rob's right. You say this 42K is good at what they do, tight-knit, shrewd. How can you have *two* informants inside?'

'I'm a PI, not a cop. I have friends who will speak to me occasionally if I offer them a few dollars. I have good contacts, who can help a man or woman out indefinitely. And I always hold up my end.'

Alicia scanned the table. Both Crouch and Caitlyn were studying Pierce with interest, fully invested in his words. They believed him, believed his tale. Russo, as befitted his personality, was sitting grumpily with his arms crossed. His face, though, was unreadable. Alicia still sat on the fence.

'How well do you know this Kalani?' she asked.

'We're good friends. Have been for years. In fact, I'm really worried for the guy and would want to find him even if he hadn't mentioned Kamehameha's tomb. Yeah, he's an idiot. He made a mistake. But then we've all been there, we've all fucked up at one time or another. Kalani shouldn't have to die because of it.'

Alicia agreed. She'd be dead a hundred times over if that were the case. 'It's not our job to search for missing people,' she said.

'But it is our job to search for buried treasure,' Crouch said. 'And they buried Kamehameha with a lot.'

Caitlyn nodded enthusiastically in agreement. 'Gold and jewels,' she said. 'Special boxes filled with coins. More than you can imagine. His tomb would be overflowing.'

Alicia had raised her eyes. 'Steady on,' she said. 'I can imagine quite a bit. I mean, we've *found* quite a bit.'

'Nothing like this,' Caitlyn told her. 'It's not the just the gold. It's the remains of the king, too.'

'Can you help me find Kalani?' Pierce asked.

'Do you have any idea where he might have gone?' Crouch asked.

'As you know, by now I'm very well connected. But here in Oahu, that doesn't matter. Kalani ran from a place north of Waikiki. He'd go to only one place. The real problem is we won't be the only people trying to track him.'

'The 42K?' Russo said.

'You got it. They know Kalani too, and they also have great island contacts. If Kalani is anything, he's too trusting. So he will mess this up.'

Alicia didn't like the sound of that. 'How long has it been since Kalani escaped?'

'A few days. He's had time to go to ground.'

'But the 42K will track him?'

'They are. My other contacts tell of a big effort on their part.'

'What would they get out of finding Kamehameha?'

'Are you kidding? They'd sell to the highest secret bidder. The people, the community, would never see the remains of the king. He'd end up in some private collection.'

'All for a few dollars,' Caitlyn shook her head in anger.

'For a *lot* of dollars,' Pierce said. 'I can't tell you how important it is that we find the treasure first, that we find Kalani first. He's important as a person, yes, but most terribly, he's actually more important as the man who knows the location of the king's tomb.'

'Is he far?' Crouch asked.

'He's still in Oahu. My spies tell me he hasn't left the island, hasn't appeared on other shores. Not yet. That's what makes me think he's gone into the forests, the hills. I know where he'd go. We've spoken about his haunts often enough.'

'The trick will be to persuade a man on the run to come in, and then lead us to the treasure,' Crouch said. 'Do you think you can do that?'

'I do,' Pierce said. 'I can convince him to do the right thing. How good are you guys at protection?'

Alicia glanced around the room. 'Pretty damn good.' The atmosphere inside the Denny's was bright and congenial, the smells wafting from the kitchen area very tempting. She could hear the rattle of plates and mugs, the tap of a waitress's heels on the floor. She laid a hand on the wooden table before her. 'We're the best at what we do.'

'The 42K are at least fifty strong,' Pierce said. 'Maybe more.'

'Nothing I can't handle after a substantial breakfast,' Russo grumbled. 'Don't worry. We got this.'

Pierce eyed them closely, as if weighing them up. Clearly, the guy needed help. He wasn't going to get this done alone. Alicia wondered how good he actually was.

She guessed she'd find out.

'Can we get the police involved?' Caitlyn asked.

For the first time, Pierce looked angry. 'You trust the cops?' he asked her directly. 'Trust them to find Kalani without putting their enormous cop feet in it? Trust them to keep the treasure secret and not flap their big cop mouths? Trust they won't blab to a few flapping ears for a few crappy dollars. Turn the find of a lifetime into a farce? Do you?'

Caitlyn held her hands up in submission. Alicia guessed there was more going on with Pierce and the police than he'd explained to them. But, essentially, he was right.

'We don't trust anyone but ourselves,' she said.

Pierce nodded. 'Then you're with me? I know your reputation. I know Michael's reputation. I'd rather have you with me than anyone else, but we have to get moving now. Right now. Kalani has been alone for days and the 42K are looking for him.'

'How do we know they haven't found him?' Caitlyn asked.

'Don't forget, I still have an informant in their gang.'

Alicia finished the last of her coffee and rose to her feet. She brushed off a few crumbs. 'What do you say, guys? Shall we go looking for some treasure?'

Crouch grinned and rose to his feet. 'The Gold team is back together. Thanks for coming, Alicia.'

'Just try to get rid of me, mate.'

'Oh, we've tried.' Russo said.

Alicia gave him the finger and headed for the exit.

CHAPTER SEVEN

To begin with, it was easy.

Pierce drove a big five-seater Chevy, bright red with black trim, which made Alicia grin when she saw it. She would have said *'Well, at least you got the colour right'* but everyone was moving way too fast. They jumped into the truck, fastened their seatbelts and sat back as Pierce started driving.

'Guns,' was the first thing that Russo said as the vehicle twisted its way through traffic. 'It sounds like we're gonna be up against a decent amount of firepower.'

'I have a gun and I have a spare,' Pierce told them. 'I'm happy to loan it to one of you.'

'I'm the best shot,' Alicia said.

Russo glared. 'Says who?'

'Says I. And I'm in charge. So just sit yourself back and accept it, Russo.'

'Not in a million years.'

'One look at an enemy and you go charging in like a rogue elephant.'

'Careful who you're calling an elephant.'

'Funny. I'd have expected a comment about the size of your trunk.'

Russo turned away from her. 'Yeah, from you maybe,' he said.

Alicia settled back for the drive. Behind them, the rear area was full of gear. All sorts of paraphernalia, from folded tents to hiking boots, from camper's pots and pans to a very large machete. There were also some outsize waterproof coats that had a kind of black, rubbery texture.

'What the hell sort of trip are you planning?' Alicia asked.

'It can be tough out there,' Pierce said. 'It certainly isn't a walk in the park.'

Alicia hadn't expected to be on the move quite as quickly. Not that it bothered her too much, but she still had her hand luggage, had no hotel, and was suffering from jetlag. Twice, she found her eyes closing in the back of the car and twice she opened them to find Russo staring at her.

'It's okay,' he said. 'You clearly need your beauty sleep.'

'So long as I can kick your arse,' Alicia grunted back. 'And I can do that with my eyes closed.'

She turned to the passing the scenery, which soon turned from the traffic-thick streets of Waikiki to green hills and a sparkling blue ocean. They left the bustle of the city behind and headed out past Diamond Head into a quieter area where men and women in pickup trucks, their vehicles loaded with surf boards, headed for beach parking areas, where tourists rambled on foot and in tour coaches, where a couple of military vehicles made their way north. Pierce kept his foot on the gas, staying just below the speed limit as he guided their car in a north-easterly direction.

'There's going to be quite a bit of walking,' he said at one point. 'As you can imagine, Kalani's hardly going to be sitting near a parking area. But I'll get us as close as we can get.'

'You sure he's gonna be there?' Caitlyn asked.

'As much as I can be. There's always a chance Kalani will choose a different place, but we've spoken many times. And this place, Palolo Point, is where he always came back to. Mount Olympus is ahead and the Wa'ahila Ridge Recreation Area, but that's maybe a bit too far. There's plenty of space between us and it. Soon, we'll be parking up. Get ready for a hike.'

Alicia stretched. Caitlyn turned to her and the two had a bit of a catch up. Apparently, Caitlyn had solved the riddle of the whereabouts of the European crown and they'd found it with little to no fuss. Also, Caitlyn had no time for a boyfriend or even getting out on a night. Alicia told her she'd have to help fix that. Caitlyn was too young to let it all pass her by.

'We're here,' Pierce said.

He pulled up in a large parking area away from the half dozen other cars that were parked there and switched off the engine. Pierce rubbed the bristle on his chin, something that seemed to be a habit. He half-turned in the driver's seat so everyone could see him.

'The trek to Palolo Point isn't easy,' he said. 'And it's pretty lawless. I realise this is Hawaii. We have police just like anywhere, but there are places on all the islands where the cops aren't welcome or just don't go. Of course, there are hiker's trails, but that doesn't mean we won't bump into someone unsavoury. Let's go with the story that I'm a local and you guys are over here, visiting. I'm showing you the sights.' Pierce reached into the glove-box and pulled out his spare gun, handing it to Alicia. 'It's a six shot,' he said unnecessarily.

Alicia palmed it and then thrust it into the back of her waistband. She cracked open the door and climbed out of the car. The red paint sparkled as the sun rose, now a shining ball in the sky.

She surveyed the terrain. Trees and foliage surrounded the parking area. There were a couple of marked trails that led out and several signposts that showed the way. She guessed they started on the easy, marked trails and then veered off later. She walked to the back of the vehicle, where Pierce was handing out provisions. He gave them water and energy bars, a hat each, and pulled out the big machete, an implement that Alicia eyed dubiously.

'Are you really gonna need that?'

'Better to have it and not need it than to need it and not have it,' Pierce replied sagely.

'If you say so,' Alicia fixed her hat on her head and watched Pierce lock the car. After that, they were ready to set out. Pierce led them to one of the marked trails, took a quick, suspicious glance around the car park, and then set off.

Alicia followed his eyes. What was he looking for? Members of the 42K? She didn't doubt that it was on his mind. The 42K were clearly cunning and versatile and could probably track Kalani just as easily as Pierce could.

The PI led them down a narrow, rutted track that twisted and turned between overhanging branches. The ground was hard and sun-baked. Alicia had remembered to bring her sunglasses and put them on now, eyes stunned by the sun that glared off the bright green foliage. As they paced along the track, the greenery grew denser and the trees formed a canopy overhead. There were no other sounds that she could hear at first, but she was hardly a Great White Hunter.

She assumed there were animals and maybe even other humans around them, but what she couldn't see didn't bother her too much.

Pierce led them through the shrubbery and between the thick boughs. An hour passed and still they followed the track. The undergrowth grew deeper still. At one point, they saw hikers on a parallel track and kept their distance, shrinking into the surrounding vegetation. The fewer people who knew they were here, the better. Pierce used a compass to make sure the path was leading them in the right direction and twice assured them that Mount Olympus was still roughly ahead, and that they were heading towards Kalani's refuge.

Another hour passed.

Finally, Pierce stopped.

'This,' he said. 'Is where us and the path part ways,' he had a topographical map in one hand, his compass in the other. 'You see, this is a hiker's path. It loops back to the parking area. Hikers are discouraged to venture beyond this point.'

'Why?' Crouch asked.

'Because it gets damn dangerous. Ready?'

'Your pep talks definitely need some practice,' Alicia grumped as she followed the PI off the main path and into the shrubbery.

Soon, they were very much lost, or would have been, if not for Pierce's trusty map. There was no simple path, no easy way between the flora that grew thickly all around. Above, the sun dappled intermittently through the overhanging canopy, bright beams of sunlight spearing their way to the ground. Alicia sweated profusely and felt her clothes sticking to her body. Her nose was filled with the smell of the surrounding scenery, her ears attuned for even the slightest sound. Birds flapped and squawked their way between trees. It might have been a pleasant journey if they weren't in a hurry to find Kalani.

Thirty minutes after Pierce led them off the track, he held up a fist. It stopped them. Pierce's body language told them to be careful. He was rigid, listening. Then, he turned quickly and waved them deeper into the surrounding plant life, directing them towards the thicker bushes and wider trees. He didn't speak, but his eyes were hard and his face was taut.

Alicia crept into a thick bush, clothes jabbed by thorns and twigs. She knelt on the ground and steadied her breathing, laid low, peering through a tangle of undergrowth. At first, she heard nothing. She was aware only of her hands bearing her weight, covered in dirt, her jeans being perforated by several sharp thorns. Already, she was dreading backing out of here.

Then, there was a noise. The sound of someone laughing. A few moments later she saw movement through the trees, the flash of colourful clothing, the waving of arms. Soon, a party of men came into sight. They were walking slowly, grouped together, and they all carried guns slung low.

Alicia was amazed. This wasn't the Amazon. It wasn't South Africa. But then she recalled what Pierce had said. Gun ownership was, of course, legal out here, and she imagined there was more than one militia group. Drug dealers and other criminals also made hard-to-reach places their homes for obvious reasons. The authorities couldn't keep track of everyone. She imagined the wilds of Oahu wasn't exactly an unpleasant place to hole up.

Her team stayed silent. She turned her head slightly, saw Caitlyn clutching a tree limb, Crouch hidden behind a mossy rock. She saw Russo hiding his bulk behind an enormous trunk, hunkered low to the ground. Pierce lay flat, his nose barely a millimetre off the ground.

The criminals – if that's what they were – passed slowly. They were chatting, laughing together and making no effort to remain unnoticed. Maybe it was just a group of locals after all. There were locals – native Hawaiians – who despised all types of foreigners and hung out signs threatening to shoot on sight if there was any kind of trespassing. It was just as possible that they considered the wilds out here their private land.

Alicia stayed low and breathed easily. After about ten minutes, the threat seemed to have passed.

She turned to Pierce. 'Onward?' she said.

The PI nodded and pushed himself up into a kneeling position. He stayed there for another minute, perhaps waiting to see if a rear guard would come along. When nothing happened, he rose to his feet and beckoned.

'Let's go,' he said.

'Who were those guys?' Caitlyn asked, brushing herself off.

'Hard to say,' Pierce said. 'But it's worrying.'

'Why's that?' Alicia asked.

'Because we're close to Kalani's hideout.'

Alicia bit her lip, worried for the young man. 'They're going the wrong way, though,' she said. 'And clearly didn't have Kalani with them.'

Pierce nodded. 'Let's hope he's okay,' he said and led the way with a grim visage.

Alicia checked her gun was in the right place and followed.

CHAPTER EIGHT

They slogged on through what felt to Alicia like a jungle.

It was hot and humid, overgrown, pierced by blinding sunlight in places, and dangerous to tread. A bumpy, narrow path veered left and right and took them down almost impossible slopes and then up inclines on the other side. A soft breeze blew through the trees, welcome on their sweating, exposed faces and arms.

Alicia kept her head down and her senses alert. They had come close earlier. It was only due to Pierce's skills that they hadn't been seen. They stayed together, Pierce leading the way, Crouch at the rear. Alicia and Russo kept an eye on their flanks.

'How far now?' Russo asked at one point.

'Not far,' Pierce replied.

'That's what you said a half hour ago.'

Up front, Pierce suddenly stopped. Alicia got closer, ready for anything. Pierce turned to her and pointed.

'See that?'

Alicia looked off to the right, maybe ten yards away from the track. She saw something in the undergrowth, something large and black. At first, she couldn't figure out what it might be, but then the reality dawned on her.

'A trap?'

Pierce nodded. 'Poachers,' he said. 'More than a few around these parts. They flourish because of the illegal trade in Honolulu. Keep it quiet.'

They walked past the trap, venturing further into the greenery. Pierce slowed down a bit later and then turned to them.

'If Kalani is here,' he said. 'We should see him soon.'

'This is the right place?' Crouch asked.

'This is the general area.'

'Couldn't he just lie quiet until we go past?' Caitlyn asked.

'Of course,' Pierce said. 'But I'm hoping when he sees me he'll make an appearance.'

Alicia thought that was some risky assumption. Kalani held the key to everything. The whole treasure hunt for Kamehameha, the resting place of the great king. Their quest was useless without Kalani.

Pierce found a clearing and started hunting around. Alicia assumed he was looking for any sign of Kalani. Even if Kalani had been the best tracker or whatever, he'd have left some sign of his passing. After several days out here, he'd have to.

Finally, Pierce straightened. He sighed and walked to the edge of the clearing. 'I fear,' he said. 'That I might have led you on a wild goose chase.'

Alicia scanned the clearing. 'He could be here,' she said. 'Could be—'

At that moment, a shadow detached itself from the surrounding foliage. Alicia saw it coming and immediately whipped her gun out. The shadow was a figure, and it paced towards Pierce.

The PI made no move for his weapon. Instead, he started grinning and held out a hand. 'My friend,' he said. 'I knew you'd be here.'

'What the hell are you doing?' Kalani asked. 'Who are these people?'

Alicia studied Kalani as he stood angrily before Pierce. He was a young man, clean-shaven, with a few tattoos and an angular face. His hair was black, his bare arms sinewy. He might try berating Pierce, but all Alicia saw was a scared kid.

'We've come here to help you,' Pierce said with an uncertain edge to his voice. 'Kalani, there are people hunting you, people who want to kill you.'

'I know,' Kalani said in exasperation. 'That's why I'm in the middle of fucking nowhere.'

'But that's why you need friends. To help you, to find the treasure with you and give them no further reason to come after you.'

'Ah, so it's the treasure you're here for.' Kalani's face twisted into regret.

Pierce laid a hand on Kalani's shoulder. 'No, my friend. I'm here to help you. But I've thought this all the way through. The 42K know you found Kamehameha. We'll get to the incredulity of that later. But, assuming you did, they won't stop until they've tortured the information out of you. And then they'll kill you.'

Kalani rubbed his face. 'I know. As soon as Lynskey finds the tomb, he'll have no further use for me.'

Pierce frowned. 'Who's Lynskey?'

'One of the 42K top dogs. A leader. The other two are called Kovats and Johnson.'

'I thought nobody knew who ran the 42K.'

Kalani shrugged. 'I found out. Insiders talk. Once you're in, it's hard for them to stay anonymous. Look, thanks for coming, Pierce, but I don't see how you can help me. And who the hell are all these people?'

Pierce introduced them one by one. 'They're here to help. I couldn't do this alone. I know the 42K won't be far behind. Have you been living out here for the last two days?'

'Almost three.' Kalani said. 'It gets easier, believe me.'

'But you can't remain here forever.'

Kalani stepped away. 'I have food, water, sustenance. I have everything I need. Maybe I can escape to one of the other islands, make a living there.'

'The 42K are too well connected,' Pierce said. 'They'd see you enter, follow you. I mean, damn, I could do the same. You know how good my connections are. How can you possibly hope to remain unnoticed?'

'I have to try.'

Pierce walked forward, grabbed Kalani's arm. 'Join us,' he breathed. 'Help us find the treasure. Doing that will get you out of this hole. They wouldn't dare touch the man who found Kamehameha's tomb. Imagine it, Kalani, you would be a celebrity. You'd be on all the talk shows; in the news.'

'Untouchable,' Kalani said, hope in his voice.

'We're treasure hunters,' Crouch said, stepping forward. 'Tom here asked us to come along to lend our support. I could guarantee you total coverage. We've done this kind of thing before.'

'I don't know you,' Kalani said.

'No, but *he* does.' Alicia pointed at Pierce. 'Crouch and him go way back. And we wouldn't come all this way not to help.'

'How do I know you're not just interested in the whereabouts of Kamehameha?'

Pierce sighed. 'You don't. You're going to have to trust me. Join us, Kalani. This will be a grand adventure.'

Kalani nodded. 'That much is true,' he said. 'Kamehameha is all but inaccessible. I guess that's why he's stayed hidden for so long.'

Crouch sat on a rock near the centre of the clearing. 'Talk to us about it.'

Pierce opened his arms. 'We're here to help. We'll keep the 42K off your back, keep you safe.'

Kalani sat down on a rock opposite Crouch. 'I knew Kamehameha's remains were hidden according to ritual,' he breathed. 'They made a special woven basket to contain his bones. The basket had eyes made of mother-of-pearl. They made the mouth of the face from Kamehameha's own teeth. It was tradition and ritual back in those days. Deep tradition. People with the names Ho'olulu, Hoapili and Keopuolani became the undertakers of the remains; they worked together after Kamehameha's death.'

'Worked to bury him?' Crouch asked.

'He's not buried. Far from it. The waters and the volcano have kept him safe.'

And right there, Alicia knew, was a clue. Hawaii might be a volcanic chain, but there weren't that many active volcanoes along its length. She kept her mouth shut.

Kalani looked nervous, perhaps realising he'd just revealed a snippet of information to them. He stared between Crouch and Pierce.

'What's your plan?'

'First, we get you out of here and back to civilisation,' Pierce said. 'Then we keep you out of sight. After that, we come up with a reveal plan. You're going to have to share Kamehameha's whereabouts with us so we can do that. And Michael here will know what to do once we complete the find, who to call, how to handle it.'

Kalani sighed deeply. 'I'll actually be quite glad to get rid of this burden,' he said. 'It's a mountain on my shoulders, weighing me down. I've struggled with it ever since I found the place and, often, I truly wish I hadn't.'

'Don't be like that,' Crouch said. 'The knowledge saved your life.'

Kalani shrugged. 'Kind of,' he said. 'It was really luck that saved my life, and stupidity. Jumping out of that first-floor window. But I couldn't stay in that room.'

'We'll keep them away from you,' Pierce reiterated.

Kalani narrowed his eyes at them. 'Thank you,' he said. 'But I don't see how you can do that. You are five people.'

'You haven't seen us in action,' Alicia said with a grim smile.

But he was about to.

Right then, the leaves all around them parted, and the shouting started.

CHAPTER NINE

The trees seemed alive.

Alicia spun in place, at first unsure what the hell was happening. She could sense Russo jumping up beside her, his bulk a great shadow to her left. Before her, several men emerged from the trees, their faces hard. They held their weapons out, pointed at Alicia and her team, and they were shouting in Hawaiian.

'Who the hell are you?' Pierce didn't back down.

'Stop,' Alicia barked into one man's face.

The newcomers didn't back down. They waved their weapons around. Some of them started speaking English with a heavy accent. Alicia counted eight of them quickly spreading out around the clearing.

The man she'd shouted at walked right up to her, yelling. She didn't back down. He had black hair and a scarred face, evil eyes. He threw out a hand, aiming to slap her across the face, but Alicia caught it. She held on as he tried to jerk it away, held on and wouldn't let go, used her strength to make him back down.

But the guy just brought his other hand up and pointed the gun at her face.

'Back off, bitch,' he snarled.

Alicia hadn't yet untucked her own gun. Now, she bunched a fist and slammed it into the centre of the man's face. His nose exploded. He yelled out in agony.

Alicia grabbed his gun arm and broke the wrist, saw the weapon fall to the floor.

The man staggered back.

Another took his place, this one also yelling.

'Who are you?' they were shouting. 'Back the fuck off or we'll kill you.'

Alicia didn't much fancy their chances if they backed off. She kicked the new guy in the groin, watched him go down. Her actions were bound to bring the confrontation to a boil, but their attackers had now dwindled from eight to six, and they were far more evenly matched.

Alicia whipped her gun out. She pointed it at another man. When he aimed his own gun back at her, she fired.

Russo yelled out something about her being crazy.

But Alicia was faster than all of them. Before her first shot took the man down, she'd fired again and then again. Bullets struck their attackers, winging them, hitting one man in the chest. There was shock and consternation on their faces.

Alicia yelled, 'You back up! Surrender to us!'

The men attacked. Bullets flew across the clearing. Kalani threw himself to the ground first, warned by some sixth sense that the shooting was about to kick off. Pierce fell to his knees and dragged his own gun out, fired back. Crouch fell and rolled against the legs of a shooter, unbalancing him. Caitlyn and Russo dived to the ground.

Flying lead laced the air. Alicia felt the tug of a bullet against her left arm but experienced no pain. It was just the passing of the slug. A man threw his knife at her. Alicia moved her head three inches, let it fly right past. Then the man was on her, grappling for her gun.

Alicia staggered back. The guy was heavy, well-muscled. He forced her back four steps before she managed to stand her ground. She had one hand around his right wrist, another on his throat. She squeezed as he sought to punch her in the ribs.

His blows landed hard. She had hold of his larynx and gripped it tighter, ignoring the pain. She felt him tremble with the effort of punching her, ignoring the death-grip she held over him.

Crouch punched upward from the floor, connecting with his opponent's groin, staggering the man. He jumped to his feet, slower than Alicia, but still fit enough to take down a young, inexperienced upstart. The kid's gun was hanging loosely. Crouch kicked it away, saw it fly through the air.

Quickly, he scrambled after it.

Pierce fired his own weapon, taking two men down. Another was too close to him, reaching for Pierce's gun, but the PI would have none of it. He was ex-military too, trained to the highest level. He hooked a foot around his opponent's ankle, whipped it out and brought him crashing to the ground. Then Pierce was on the man, gun under his chin, telling him to give it up.

Alicia looked up. There were no more attackers on their feet. Many were lying on the ground, others were struggling with Pierce and now Russo. She manhandled her opponent, dragging him around and then pushing him away from her. When he staggered back, she followed up with a running kick to the chest. The blow made him stagger faster so that he fell backwards onto the ground.

Alicia could have shot him then, but she held off. Instead, she twisted her way around his neck and choked him until he passed out. When she looked up, she saw Russo doing the same to his own opponent and Pierce standing over a man with his gun levelled. Pierce was telling the man to stop struggling.

Alicia blinked, scanning left and right.

Where the hell was Kalani?

The fight had taken up all their attention and, during that time, Kalani had vanished. Frustration and surprise lit up Alicia's brain. She felt that they'd won Kalani over, that he'd trusted them to some small degree. And Pierce knew him. Why the hell had Kalani bolted?

She scanned the clearing once more, not trusting her eyes. Pierce was already looking at her.

'He's gone,' he said.

'What? Who?' Russo said, enormous arms still around his opponent's throat.

Crouch rose to his feet. 'Kid's scared,' he said. 'Doesn't know who to trust. He may well know you, Pierce, but he sure doesn't know us. I think we intimidated him.'

Pierce shook his head, unsure and unhappy. 'Kalani is in terrible danger,' he said. 'Whether or not he wants to admit it, whether or not he wants to face it. The 42K will learn from this loss and come back stronger.'

'They sure want the treasure,' Caitlyn said.

Alicia listened to them talk. They were way out in the Hawaiian wilds here, and it was a long way back. She wondered if they could track Kalani and asked aloud.

Pierce stared at her. 'I may be a private investigator, but I'm no tracker. I couldn't find a footprint at a surf championship on a wet beach.'

'Which means we've lost him,' Alicia said glumly.

'You mean *you* can't track?' Russo finally stood up and regarded her with mock incredulity. 'The great Alicia Myles? Mind you, that nose looks a bit too crooked for sniffing out clues.'

'I broke it a while back.'

'Did you put it back together yourself?' He grimaced.

'No, the doctors did it. Now, stop winding me up and concentrate on the problem. Without Kalani, we're dead in the water.'

'Not necessarily,' Pierce said. 'You forget who you're with.'

Alicia stared at him. 'What's that supposed to mean?'

'Oh, did I not tell you? I'm the best private detective in the world and my speciality is finding people.'

CHAPTER TEN

Kalani wished he'd never fallen into the criminal lifestyle.

There had to be a better way. There *was* a better way. Kalani just hadn't found it yet. His life had now taken a major U-turn.

Kalani ran lightly, almost skipping through the forest, careful to leave no trace behind. He didn't know who might track him – Pierce's new friends or the 42K, but he wanted nothing to do with any of them. He was scared. He had the biggest secret in the world. And suddenly everyone wanted to be his friend.

But Kalani was no fool.

Oh, no, he knew why they wanted him. The surprise element was Pierce. Kalani had always liked Pierce, and even trusted the man.

A particularly difficult patch of terrain interrupted Kalani's train of thought. He had to concentrate on the land, on his feet, on the way ahead. It wouldn't do to fall here and break a leg. You would die. And you would die badly.

Once through it, Kalani ran. He didn't need a compass. He knew these lands intimately, knew most of the islands just as well. He'd spent a lot of time out here. He loved it; the only downside being there was no TV.

Kalani loved TV. He was a connoisseur of the crime and cop shows. Things like NCIS and CSI, MacGyver and Magnum. He employed their expertise in everyday life, wondered what the main character might do in any situation. Yes, he knew it was all make believe, but Kalani liked the characters and trusted that they would do the right thing.

Take now, for instance. What would MacGyver do, stranded in the wilds with no food, no water, and an entire gang looking for him? Well, he would stay mobile. Maybe build a car out of logs. Take it to the nearest ranch and work himself out a plan. Kalani wasn't that adept yet, but he would do his best.

He forged on, sweeping past trees and undergrowth, running through clearings, trying to stay off the main trails. Twice, he encountered people, but avoided them by pressing deeper into the forest and staying silent. Twice, they passed him by, none the wiser. Neither of the encounters involved the 42K or Pierce's group. Kalani thought the first party was poachers, the second a few local drug dealers. These people used Hawaii's beautiful, remote environment to ply their trades, to hunt and concoct their poisons, and Kalani hated them for it. They destroyed the natural resources for their own gain, ignored the traditions to make a few bucks.

He waited until they'd passed and journeyed on. He headed west, back in the direction of Waikiki, but he did not know how he would get there. Not yet.

Two minutes later, Kalani fell to the floor.

There was a rush through the forest, a blundering of undergrowth and leaves and twigs. Kalani heard them some way off and was easily concealed by the time they came rampaging through. He recognised the two men, escapees from the fight in the clearing. Members of the

42K. Only they didn't look so tough now, running and sweating and bleeding and casting scared glances over their shoulders. They raced right past him and didn't notice, so intent were they on their own plights.

Kalani had to smile to himself.

Well done, Pierce, he thought.

Why had he run from the man? First, it was clear Pierce's team had been tracked. How else could the 42K had arrived on the scene like they did? Second, they had turned up out of exactly nowhere, right after he found the treasure. Would Magnum have trusted them? Kalani didn't think so. Magnum would have investigated their asses.

But Kalani didn't have that luxury. All he had was his knowledge of the islands and his many friends. He remembered the phone in his pocket and wondered who to call. That was his way out of here. He had to trek to an accessible area and then call someone with a truck, someone who could drive him back to civilisation.

Because Kalani had a new plan.

CHAPTER ELEVEN

Alicia stomped around the clearing, severely pissed off.

'You hunt people? Don't you think you might have told us that before?'

Pierce shrugged. 'There's a lot about me you don't know. And you're not really annoyed with me. You're annoyed because you lost Kalani.'

Alicia span to face him. '*I* lost him?'

'You blame yourself,' Pierce said shrewdly.

Alicia took a breath. This was getting them nowhere. 'Look,' she said. 'I assume the next move is to get our asses back to reality. Shall we get the fuck going?'

They all straightened, rubbing away their aches and pains and their pulled muscles. If the fight hadn't been hard enough, it was a long marathon to get back to the parking area. It would take a while and, Alicia knew, all that time Kalani would get further and further away.

'If he doesn't want our help...' she said once they had resumed their trek.

'Cut him loose?' Pierce eyed her. 'Not an option. Kalani's a friend, and he's being exploited by a criminal gang. They'll likely kill him. I don't blame him for running.'

Alicia tended to agree, though she was in an argumentative mood and didn't want to admit it to Pierce.

'The real question is... what would he do next?'
Crouch stayed coherent in his thought processes,
unlike Alicia.

'Great question,' Pierce said pointedly. 'That's where
we're really at. I know Kalani. Where would he go?
What would he do? All good points. And I have an
idea.'

As they trekked back, Pierce pulled his mobile
phone from his pocket. He held it up in the air,
searching for a signal, then sighed and put it away. Ten
minutes later, he did the same thing and then again,
ten minutes after that. Finally, as they approached the
parking area, hot and sweaty and tired, he let out a
grunt of victory and started tapping the buttons on his
phone.

'Alana, is that you? It's Tom Pierce here. How the
hell are you?'

The answer must have come back in the affirmative,
because Pierce ploughed straight ahead. 'Listen, you
know Kalani? He's in trouble, and I'm trying to find
him. Has he come to you for help?' Pierce was relying
on his own reputation to garner the help of his
associates. It was a risky move, but what else could he
do?

Alana wasn't in the know. Pierce then moved on to
another contact, a man named Halia, and gave him the
same spiel. Still nothing. Pierce worked through his
contacts, stopping when they reached the car and
taking out a bottle of water that he finished before
continuing. Alicia checked her watch. It was 16.30,
twenty-seven degrees, and breezy. The skies were clear
blue, allowing the hot Hawaiian sun to glare right
down on them. She shrugged her own backpack off her
shoulders, removed food and drink and ate it perched

on a bench. The others sat around her in silence, doing the same.

They waited for Pierce to continue.

It was a sombre half hour. Pierce made at least a dozen calls, many of whom said they'd call him back. By the time he'd finished, his eyes were hard, his face severe.

'That's the first batch,' he said. 'I'll wait a while before I call the rest.'

'You know a few people, then?' Russo said.

'As I said before, I know everyone who matters. Someone will help Kalani. It's just a matter of finding the right person.'

'And hoping he helps you?'

'They'll help me. I have faith.'

Alicia had no option but to get on board with Pierce's plan. She still thought Kalani had done the wrong thing and found it hard to follow the kid's thought processes. Why would he run away from a friend into the empty wilderness? Why run alone? How could he hope to evade the 42K?

Of course, Kalani wasn't exactly level headed, she thought. He wouldn't have touched the criminal game if he was, wouldn't have got involved. Alicia thought he was a very confused man who made a lot of bad choices and then, somehow, miraculously stumbled across the greatest treasure in Hawaiian history. It was an odd, but cool story, but maybe Kalani didn't see it that way.

They finished their food, emptied their bottles of water. The parking area was busy now, cars of all descriptions coming and going and hikers filling up the empty spaces. A coach full of tourists rumbled slowly by. No doubt there was a tour guide on board telling all about ecosystems and Kualoa, the Oahu valleys and Jurassic Park.

Alicia felt the passage of time weighing her down. She wasn't a woman who liked to stay in one place for too long. She walked over to Pierce, who perched lightly on the front of their car.

'Any luck?'

'Not yet. I'm expecting a call back.'

As he spoke, his phone rang. He raised his eyebrows at her, fished it out of his pocket, and answered. 'Hey?'

Alicia could hear the other guy's tinny voice through the speaker.

'Pierce? It's Iona. Can you speak?'

'Yeah, I'm good. Do you have something for me?'

'Sorry, man, but it's all about the money. Do you have anything?'

Pierce closed his eyes briefly and then looked over at Crouch. 'We good at offering a reward for information?'

Crouch nodded. 'Not too much.'

Pierce grasped the phone tighter. 'I got some, bro. Depends how good your information is.'

'It's as good as it gets. Friend of mine helped Kalani out of Palolo. Drove him for miles. Kalani didn't say much during the journey, but my friend was worried about him. Looked like he'd been in a fight. Kalani wouldn't tell him much, but he did let on that he wasn't staying in Oahu.'

Pierce frowned. 'You're kidding?'

'Nah, bro, not at all. Kalani was scared.'

'I can imagine he would be. But I hope you have more for me than that, Iona.'

'Sure I do. I'm worth the green. When they reached Waikiki, Kalani got more talkative. Excited even. He spoke of fading away.'

Pierce knit his brows even further. Alicia didn't like the sound of that.

'Fading away?' Pierce repeated. 'What the hell does that mean?'

'He's going to ground, man. Plugging out of the network.'

'Where?'

'And that's where the money comes in. I can tell you, but it has to be a thousand.'

Pierce snorted. 'No way am I giving you a thousand. The info's worth two hundred, max. I can make it up to you in other ways. Don't forget what I can do.'

Alicia assumed a man as connected as Pierce could put good words in for Iona across the islands. Sometimes, a good word was worth far more than reward. She leaned forward, listening intently for the next words.

'Two hundred, then. Listen, I'm sticking my neck out by doing this, betraying my friend's trust. You make sure you come through for me, Pierce.'

'I will.'

'All right. Kalani said he was going to find someone to take him to Kauai. As fast as possible. Straight from Waikiki or Honolulu to Kauai. He has somewhere he can go over there, apparently.'

Pierce nodded. 'I recall him telling me about a place he liked to haunt. Similar to what he had in Palolo. Out of the way, quiet, hard to find. But, man, doesn't he realise he will still have to show his face to collect supplies?'

The last sentence was a frustrated outburst, Alicia knew. And she knew why Pierce made it. It was because the 42K had just as many eyes and ears across the islands as Pierce did. If Pierce could track him down, the 42K could. It might just take them a little longer.

'You know Kalani,' Iona laughed. 'He's probably watched how to grow his own pasta on one of those cop shows he loves so much.'

Pierce thanked Iona, promised he'd get his money soon, then hung up and regarded the team. Alicia took a moment to study them too. Crouch was looking expectant, ready to move at a moment's notice, eager to get started properly on their treasure hunt. Russo just looked big and immovable, his big forehead creased with irritation. Caitlyn was moving from foot to foot, apparently ready to start her research at any moment. Alicia knew that she'd be swotting up on Kamehameha at every opportunity.

'It's a good lead.' Pierce said.

'I'm ready to go,' Caitlyn said. 'The only way to do a treasure hunt is to immerse yourself in it up to the neck.'

Crouch gave Pierce a thumbs up. 'I'm happy to follow your lead with this. My team is yours.'

Alicia looked at Russo and raised an eyebrow. 'You happy with that, Rob?'

'I'm not happy with anything. You should know that by now.'

'Well, it looks like we're going on a boat journey,' Alicia said. 'How far is Kauai, anyway?'

'Not a boat,' Pierce told them. 'I have access to a plane.'

Alicia was impressed. 'You really are Magnum.'

'It's not fancy. And they might not allow us to use it. And we'll have to pay for the fuel.'

'I take it all back,' Alicia said.

But Crouch was already in motion. 'We don't have a moment to lose,' he said.

CHAPTER TWELVE

Kalani loved Kauai. In his opinion, it was the most beautiful of the Hawaiian islands, the most diverse, most versatile. It suited his needs perfectly.

Clearly, the situation was too hot on Oahu. He needed to get away, to get off, and this was the perfect way to do it. He'd relied on a friend to get him to Honolulu, where a small plane was about to take off for Kauai. Kalani knew the pilot very well and, luckily for him, there was a spare seat on the plane. The downside was that Kalani had nothing with him, no belongings apart from a mobile phone and a wallet that contained his dwindling funds and a debit and credit card. He knew all about CCTV and computer tracing from the cop shows, so wouldn't be using the cards anytime soon. But the cash would last him a while.

He hopped from one island to the next, perfectly happy once he'd landed on Kauai and taken a taxi to Lihue, from where he could later set out on his journey. There was a slight rain shower that soaked him to the bone and then the sun came out again, gloriously strong, and made his clothes steam. Kalani used his time in Lihue to purchase a sturdy rucksack, enough food and water to last for several days, and made sure his phone was as charged up as he could get it.

He walked steadily from shop to shop, keeping his head down. He knew the 42K had spies everywhere, but it would be bad luck if they saw him here, right now, in the small window of time he had allowed himself to purchase supplies.

Once done, Kalani headed out of town.

It hadn't always been this way, he mused as he walked. Once there had been an uncle who took him everywhere. Old Jace, as he was called, had a rugged pickup truck, once blue, but washed grey by the Hawaiian sun and the conditions where he drove it. It didn't matter whether or not there was a road, whether or not there was a *trail*, Old Jace used to take that pickup down it, with Kalani bouncing along in the passenger seat, laughing out loud and clinging on for dear life.

They were good years. Kalani did well in school. His uncle ran a car workshop, and he ran it well. He was a busy guy. During the evenings, Kalani used to join him there, to help tinker with whatever he was working on. This was where Kalani started building up a network of contacts by talking incessantly to every customer who came through the door. Old Jace wasn't a talker. He was a ponderer, a thinker. Often, to Kalani's amusement, he would blurt out an answer to a question three days later.

But Old Jace was prone to spontaneous bouts of action and often took Kalani out into the wilds, just as often as he would take him to the zoo or the mall. It was the impulsivity of it that Kalani liked, the sense that you never really knew what you were going to do that day, or where you would end up.

It all instilled a sense of the unplanned within Kalani, made him become a kind of flighty guy. Kalani had no foot in the bedrock of life, no role model other than his uncle. And where his young life was fun and instinctive, it didn't give him a responsible foundation. He grew up unruly at school, disobedient as a youth, but respectful and friendly. He was an enigma to his friends, but a likeable one.

Kalani's fall from grace came when his uncle died. It came out of the blue, a car accident that saw a drunk driver smashing into Old Jace's car head on, pushing it off the road and sending it hurtling down a cliff. It was unknown whether Jace died from the initial impact or the fall, but, right then and there, Kalani believed that his life was done.

He saw the drunk driver in court, leapt over the benches and took hold of his throat, tried to strangle him to death. The guards dragged Kalani off before he did any damage, but the rage never diminished. It ate Kalani up from the inside, took away anything that stimulated him. He found weed, found that it took the edge off, found that his friends would sell it to him at a discount because of who he was.

Kalani realised he was a well-liked figure in many communities.

He travelled; he stayed out in the wilds for weeks on end, grew used to the lifestyle. He never learned to live off the land because he always took supplies with him. It didn't matter which island. Kalani grew used to them all. Of course, a lifestyle like his required money to fund it. Kalani knew people who could get him jobs; he could get a job every day of the week. The trouble was, he didn't like any of them, didn't feel content making a Jamba Juice or cooking at the Cheesecake Factory; didn't feel comfortable parking cars and didn't have the skills to teach people how to surf or swim or paddle.

Through friends, he heard the 42K gave good money to anyone who would transport items between places without asking questions. How hard could that be? Kalani swore he would never get sucked into the world and gave it a try. From that moment, it was the ease of his job that sucked him in. Steadily, he met more and more of the 42K, even became friendly with some of them.

That all felt like a long time ago. The experiences had shaped Kalani, made him the man he was today.

And that man was running scared.

Darkness had fallen by the time Kalani left Lihue, his backpack full of provisions. Yes, he knew where he was going, but he stopped along the way, not risking too much in the gathering dark. He was safe now, safe here on Kauai, far away from the 42K and Tom Pierce and his new strange friends.

The question of Kamehameha remained.

What am I going to do?

Kalani was so absorbed in his thinking that he never saw the figures behind him, the shadows that merged mostly with the night. Never heard them. Never sensed them.

But they followed him all the way from Lihue.

CHAPTER THIRTEEN

Kalani was on Kauai!

It was great news and galvanised the team. They jumped into their vehicle and drove swiftly from the parking area all the way through Waikiki and on to Honolulu. The traffic was still dense at this time of night, denser than Alicia had ever seen it. Through Waikiki they crawled from traffic light to traffic light, surrounded by a sea of red brake lights. Pierce pushed it as fast as he dared, constantly rubbing his stubble, and, when Russo offered to drive, told him that if you didn't know the local streets, there were too many ways to become a cropper on Oahu – many one-way streets and even some one-way streets that reversed direction half way down.

It was getting dark by the time they arrived at a private airport. Alicia, seated on the left side of the car, watched the volcanic glow in the sky embrace the western horizon before slipping out of sight behind a distant shore.

Pierce pulled up in a dedicated parking space. 'All out,' he said. 'Time to get lucky.'

They leapt from the car and ran to a small plane. It still wasn't completely dark. People peered out of the windows, probably having paid to take a night-flight over the islands. Alicia and the others ran up the steps into the plane and buckled into their seats.

'Sorry we're late!' Alicia shouted to the other passengers. 'Emergency.' That would get them thinking.

Ten minutes later, they were airborne. Alicia saw the glittering lights of Oahu through the plane's right window as it banked into the night, flying for the darkness. The great crater of Diamond Head reared up, silhouetted against the greyer sky at its back. The drone of the engines interrupted her train of thought.

Alicia sat forward and tapped Pierce on the shoulder. 'Do we know where to go once we get there?'

'Kalani spoke about it often. I just need a local map. A good one.'

This treasure hunting business was a pain in the arse, she decided. Always chasing their tails from one location to another, always chasing something that felt ages-old, wraith-like, nothing more than a dusty old legend. It was hard, thankless work. It weighed down on her until... until that was, they found the treasure.

She loved that moment, was intoxicated by it. All the bad sloughed away to be replaced by something enchanting and far more pleasant. The very act of treasure hunting got right down in your blood. It held on to you, gripping with wondering fingers. That was why, whenever Crouch called, Alicia was on the very next plane out.

She hung on now as the plane descended towards the island of Kauai. It was an abrupt descent, and a steep one, sending her heart up into her mouth, but soon the little plane's tyres were skidding and bouncing their way across a runway, the plane was taxiing, and then the doors were being opened to allow the team out.

'Just a little detour, folks,' the captain was placating those who had paid for a tour. 'Won't take more than a minute.'

Alicia climbed out of the plane with a wave at the tourists. Outside, the air was warm, a balmy Hawaiian night. She walked across the asphalt and into a hangar where they went through some minor security and then found a rental car waiting for them on the other side.

Pierce took the wheel.

'Frome here, we drive to Lihue,' he said. 'Sit back. It's about thirty minutes.'

Darkness had fallen fully. They were about fifteen minutes into their drive when Pierce cleared his throat and then started talking.

'Folks,' he said. 'We have a problem.'

Crouch sat forward. 'What's wrong?'

'We can't go looking for Kalani in the dark. Apart from the obvious, that he'd hear us coming a mile off, we can't see in the damn dark and I can't find my way.'

It had already occurred to Alicia, but she'd stayed tight-lipped. 'So you're saying we're all gonna have to get a room together?' she flashed a smile at Russo.

'Over my dead carcass,' he grumbled.

'I can arrange that,' Alicia said.

'Yes,' Pierce said, unhappy. 'But don't worry, I—'

'Know someone,' Caitlyn finished for him. 'Yeah, we know.'

They drove on in silence for a while. Then, as lights appeared in the distance, Pierce found an all-night diner and pulled over into the parking area. He took his phone out and made a couple of calls. By the time he'd finished, he had them holed up at the nearest Marriott with free dinner and free breakfast, ocean view rooms and a direct line to the concierge. Pierce was nothing if he wasn't useful.

'The PI life doesn't exactly appear to be a tough one,' Alicia said when he told them.

'It could be worse,' Pierce agreed. 'I've found that it's who you know and who you treat right that gets you ahead in this world.'

They drove right to the front doors of the Marriott and gave their keys to the valet. Alicia found herself stepping out of the car into the clement night, her face caressed by warm winds, the sound of the ocean lapping at the shores in the air. Golden lights lit up the front of the hotel. They passed into the air-conditioned lobby and went straight up to the reception desk, grabbed the key cards for their rooms, and arranged to meet in thirty minutes.

Alicia threw her bag into her room. They hadn't brought any weapons with them, preferring not to risk it between the islands, so she didn't have to take care of that. She felt frustrated knowing that Kalani was out there, and that the people hunting for Kalani were also out there. If they captured Kalani, there was no telling what they would do to him. And, although she'd only met him for a short while, she felt Kalani was a good kid. Just forced into difficult lifestyle choices, some of them not his own fault, some of them the fault of others. It was the same for some kids the world over, but if Alicia didn't feel bad for them, who would?

She showered, changed clothes, and sat on the bed for a while, thinking. She wondered if some of them – namely her and Russo – should look at taking the 42K out directly, at source. The extra heat would give them something to think about, maybe divert attention from the hunt for Kalani. It was a thought anyway. Maybe she'd talk to Crouch about it later.

Alicia rose from the bed and made her way down to the lobby. She met up with Caitlyn and followed her into the restaurant where the others were already seated. Alicia ordered a beer and sat back to wait, listening to the ambient conversation, gazing through the far glass windows that overlooked the black ocean outside.

'The good news is that the bad guys are in the same boat,' Pierce was saying. 'No way can they go crashing about in the darkness out there. It's too dangerous.'

'But they might try,' Caitlyn said.

'I hope so,' Pierce said. 'It'll be less for us to take car of when the time comes.'

'You think they'll find Kalani again?' Crouch asked.

'The trouble is – lowlife elements of the same network that I use could double their money selling the criminals the same information. They probably will, and there's no getting around it. If we don't come up against the 42K again, I'd be very surprised.'

Alicia ordered steak and chips from the waiter, preferring to stick with something she knew. Around her, the conversation continued.

'Any ideas how Kalani might have stumbled across King Kamehameha's tomb?' Crouch asked. It was a typical question from Crouch, something that personified their staunch, treasure-hunting leader.

Pierce shrugged. 'Only that Kalani ventures across these islands like a tireless wind. Every week, he's somewhere different, camping out, living free. He's a free spirit and probably knows more about these lands than most local tour guides. I guess he just knows his way around. People like that, they tend to explore.'

'And he got mega lucky,' Russo said.

'Probably that too,' Pierce said. 'We all need a little luck in our lives.'

The conversation turned. It was an odd night, fraught with tension. Not tension between them, but something mixed with fear for Kalani and frustration over the time they were losing. Alicia couldn't settle, not even when she finished her third beer. She didn't say much, and neither did Russo. Maybe he was wrapped up in his own feelings, too.

She slept fitfully and woke to the alarm at 5.45 a.m. Pierce had told them that sunrise was at 6.48 that day, so they wanted to get breakfast and be ready to depart as the sun blessed the sky. They breakfasted and were heading out towards the car as the chill of night still hung over the day. Pierce swung the keys in his left hand. Together, they found the car in the parking area and got in. Now Pierce spread his map over the dashboard.

'There,' he said, jabbing his finger at a place Alicia couldn't see. 'This entire area would be Kalani's haunt. It's a few square miles, so we're gonna have to get lucky, but I think if we make ourselves obvious, Kalani might come to us.'

'You think we made a good impression on him back on Oahu?' Crouch asked.

'I think I still have his trust.'

'Let's hope you're right,' Caitlyn said.

They set off with the sunrise appearing glorious inch by inch. Alicia sat back, resting, conserving her energy. They did not know what was about to happen. Would Kalani greet them? Would he be pleased to see them, or would he hide away? Were the 42K already on the scene?

Pierce drove them along a few twisting roads and then through some foothills. They left Lihue and the Marriott far behind. An hour passed. Finally, Pierce pulled off into some remote parking area similar to the one they'd used yesterday and switched off the car.

'Not so bad today,' he said. 'Twenty minutes hiking, I guess.'

They exited the car, shrugged on their backpacks replete with provisions, and set off on their journey. Pierce stopped them about fifteen minutes later.

'Slow down,' he said.

Alicia had already seen the party ahead of them, but they had passed several hikers already on the trail and she'd dismissed their presence.

But Pierce's next words sent a bolt of trepidation through her body.

'I recognise two of those guys,' he said. 'They must have had the same idea as us. They're 42K.'

CHAPTER FOURTEEN

With no sign of Kalani in the vicinity, the team had to slow down.

Alicia watched the members of the 42K as they wound their way through the undergrowth. As far as she could see, they numbered nine, and were all focused on the way ahead, most of them not liking what they were doing, judging by their body language. Alicia knew that, for now, they should keep their distance.

'What do we do?' Caitlyn asked.

Crouch didn't take his eyes off the gang members. 'We stay quiet. We follow. Pierce, I assume this is the right direction?'

The PI nodded. 'They're on the perfect route to dissect Kalani's roaming area. But that doesn't mean they'll find him.'

'I should say not,' Alicia said. 'He's far more experienced at this than they are.'

'Maybe they're gonna flush him out,' Russo said.

'How would they do that?'

'By yelling, by shooting into the undergrowth, by chasing him down. Is there anything or anyone alive that Kalani loves?'

Pierce looked back. 'I know what you're saying. Coercion. But no, Kalani is completely alone.'

The team trod lightly and carefully, keeping the 42K in sight, but only just. It was when Pierce told them they were nearing Kalani's general site they had to slow down even more. It was clear the 42K knew exactly where they were going.

'We have no weapons,' Alicia pointed out.

'Of course we do.' Russo shook his head at her. 'Plenty. Only, they're currently in the hands of our enemies.'

It was a fair point. Alicia nodded at the big man.

Russo blinked at her. 'I have an idea,' he said.

Alicia's face fell. 'Fuck me,' she said. 'I guess even a Tyrannosaurus had an idea once in it's life.'

Russo waved them to gather around. 'I'll explain quickly,' he said. 'In my unit, in the army, we would call it a Ghraib, because most of the troops involved in it came from the Abu Ghraib base. Basically, we sneak up on our marching enemy, using our skills, from the rear and take them out one at a time. By the time those in front know we're there, they're down to the last one or two.'

Alicia knew the manoeuvre. She'd performed it countless times before. 'In this scenario, I like it,' she said. 'The forest will help conceal our actions. The dinosaur done good.'

Russo ignored her. He was already moving quickly, grim determination written all over his face. Alicia pursued him, motioning to the others to stay back.

'I want to help,' Pierce said. 'I was army too, remember?'

'The fewer people involved, the better,' Alicia said. 'Let Russo and I take care of this.'

She moved with swift feet, soon catching up to Russo. Together, they slipped through the foliage and between trees, treading lightly. The nine men in front of them were nicely spread out and moving carefully, watching every angle except their rear. When one man – a guy wearing wraparound sunglasses and sporting a goatee – turned around, Alicia and Russo were quick to duck under cover.

It took them fifteen minutes to creep into place. By that time, Alicia was in front, and just inches away from her target. The 42K goon did not know she was there. He was just another villain creeping through the forest that she could reach out and tap on the shoulder.

She chose her moment well. This man was at the back of the pack. As he made his way around a large tree, she rose, hooked an arm around his throat, and dragged him down into the foliage. She pressed hard across his larynx, cutting off his air supply. Soon the guy would pass out from lack of air. She didn't let up, counting the seconds, feeling the fight go out of his body.

She left him in their wake.

Russo was up next, closing in on his target. Alicia saw his massive bulk emerge from the undergrowth like a dark avenging angel, close over a smaller figure, and drag it down to the ground. There was no sound, no signs of a scuffle. It looked like the man simply disappeared, gone one minute, in hell the next.

Alicia had been pacing towards the scene. Two of them were down now. She'd made sure she relieved her enemy of his gun, a small Glock with just seven bullets remaining, and had tucked it into her waistband. Now she passed the scene of Russo's struggle and closed in on the next man.

This one would be tougher.

There were two of them, walking alongside each other. She would need Russo's help for this. She slowed, looked back, waited for him, and then showed him the next scenario. He nodded silently. Together, they passed along the forest floor, making no noise and slipping between branches and over soft foliage. They paced softly, getting closer and closer to their enemies.

When the time was right, they reared up together, each took hold of their opponent around the neck and hauled them to the ground. Alicia spent half a minute choking her man before he passed out. Russo's took a little longer.

They rose. They had to act fast. They'd taken down four opponents so far, but that still left five active enemies, all armed. Alicia knew that the ones they'd choked out wouldn't stay unconscious for long, either. But she didn't want to kill them. It was a race against time. She took another gun, stuffed that into her belt where it sat uncomfortably. If she was going to procure any more handguns, she was going to have to find a bigger pair of trousers.

They moved on, still creeping, still silent. Behind them, their companions moved at a slower pace, staying out of sight.

And then it all changed.

One of the 42K, the man in the lead, started shouting, yelling at the top of his voice, and then he started shooting, firing bullets left and right into the undergrowth. He spoke Hawaiian, but Alicia thought he sounded frustrated. Most likely, he was sick of the hike and was ordering Kalani to show himself.

The trouble was, the rest of the group then looked back to see how their colleagues were doing.

Alicia saw it coming and slipped behind a tree. She heard a shout of incredulity that then turned to query and then warning. More shots rang out. The 42K were definitely a jumpy bunch. Alicia waited until the shooting died away.

She looked out as a figure passed her tree. They almost bumped heads. Alicia's right hand shot out, grabbed the man's wrist and broke it, making him drop the gun he was carrying. He didn't cry out, but wrenched himself away, whipping out a knife with his good hand.

It forced Alicia to show herself. She stepped out from the concealment of the tree, blocked the man's knife thrust and then shot him in the stomach. He went down with a grasp, still holding on to the knife.

Russo fired at the same time as Alicia. His bullet thudded into a thick branch just a millimetre to the left of a man's head. The guy jumped in shock and then returned fire. Bullets thudded through the trees.

'Where the hell is Kalo? Napa? Kai?' someone was going through the names of the men they'd already felled. Someone who sounded scared.

The 42K were down to four men.

But they were concealed now, and aware that they were under attack. The bright Hawaiian sun, rising and spearing the treetops, shone down on a tense scene. Alicia heard the others creep up to them and hunker down.

They could hear the criminals talking.

'Lynskey,' one of them said. 'What the hell's going on?'

Alicia perked up at the sound of the name. Wasn't Lynskey one of the leaders of the 42K?

'Don't call me that,' the one called Lynskey growled back. 'And how the hell should I know?'

'Is it Kalani?'

'What? Taking down five men? I don't think so, do you?'

Alicia watched. She drew a bead on the nearest attacker and fired. The bullet shaved splinters off the tree next to the man's head and made him scramble down further, but not before she saw droplets of blood flying. She'd trimmed his face with the tree.

'Who are you?' the one called Lynskey called out. 'We don't want any trouble? We're just here to find our friend.'

Alicia was thinking quickly. This standoff wouldn't do. Not only were they in a stalemate with the 42K, Kalani would surely already be running again, having heard the gunfire. He'd know they were here, searching for him.

'Why don't you come out?' Lynskey shouted. 'We can talk.'

Alicia waved her gun at him. 'I'm coming out,' she said.

CHAPTER FIFTEEN

She held up her hand and moved out into the open. Instantly, four guns opened fire. Alicia was ready for it. She dived forward, hitting the ground and rolling. With the bad guy's attention focused on Alicia, Russo and Pierce, both armed, stepped out and started firing. Their bullets laced the clearing, shredding leaves and twigs, smashing into trees and branches and passing through the foliage.

One of the 42K screamed in agony.

Alicia crawled forward at a fast pace. She stayed as low as she could, closing the gap on the man called Lynskey. Maybe, if they could grab him, they could stop the 42K in their tracks.

But she wasn't as direct as Tom Pierce.

The PI suddenly dashed past her, intent on attacking Lynskey. There was something in his face, something nasty that she hadn't seen before. Pierce ate up the ground and, as Russo continued to fire, stopped at the tree where Lynskey was hiding and pulled the man out into the open.

He growled, 'You bastard. I know you.'

Russo stopped shooting, scared of hitting Pierce.

Alicia rose quickly, punching out at another gang member. The guy covered up and took the punches. She concentrated on his face and throat, trying to take him down, but the guy seemed to have some boxing experience and knew how to defend himself.

Pierce swung an arm at Lynskey. By all accounts, he was one of the three bosses of the 42K. He blocked Pierce's blow and sent back three of his own.

Pierce staggered. Lynskey brought the gun up.

'And you'll die knowing it,' Lynskey hissed.

There was a gunshot. Pierce shuddered. The part of the tree beside his head exploded. The shot had come from Crouch. It sent Lynskey diving for cover, having not fired his weapon. Pierce shook himself and jumped onto Lynskey's back.

'Bastard!' he yelled. *'You bastard! You're supposed to be better than this!'*

Alicia didn't know what to say or what to think. Her opponent flew at her, still with his gun in one hand but using it as a battering ram. Alicia ducked, but the gun hit her across the top of her head. For a moment, she saw stars. She staggered. The guy brought up a knee that just missed her nose. A stroke of luck she was extremely thankful for. Since she was already low, she went lower, falling to her knees and concentrating her blows on the guy's midriff and groin. He yelled out and fell in front of her so that, suddenly; they were face to face.

'How's yer balls?' she asked.

And with that, she head-butted him full in the face, heard his cry and watched him fall over amid a great gout of blood. His nose had broken, and he was out like a light. Alicia relieved him of his weapon and held it in her hand.

Looked around.

The 42K was dwindling fast. They would only be three strong now, including Lynskey. Pierce was still yelling in the man's face, his anger preventing him from using his skills to the max. Lynskey twisted out of his grip, leapt to his feet and aimed a kick at Pierce's skull.

The boot struck hard. Pierce fell backwards. Lynskey cried out to his men and ran off into the forest.

Alicia saw the remaining 42K members melt away among the trees. That was perfect for now.

'Where the hell is Kalani?' Crouch was shouting.

'He'll have hightailed it out of here by now,' Russo said angrily.

But Alicia was running for Pierce. 'What were you talking about? What did you mean? Did you recognise Lynskey?'

Pierce dragged himself to her side. He was holding his right cheek where Lynskey had booted it and where, already, there was a mottled bruise blossoming.

'Yeah, I recognised the bastard,' Pierce grunted.

'Who was he?'

Pierce's face turned into a snarl. 'He's a fucking cop,' he said.

CHAPTER SIXTEEN

Kalani saw them coming.

He didn't have much time. It had been a good night, a soundless, relaxing kip under the stars, wrapped in a blanket and with his provisions by his side. Kalani had slept in the hollow of a high hill, surrounded by trees and bushes and undergrowth and clumps of grass. He'd spent the first part of the night staring up at the cloudless skies, revelling in the peace and quiet and the majestic beauty that was Hawaii. It moved him, made him feel special and comfortable with life. It was exactly the rest and comfort he needed after the past twenty-four hours or so.

The morning had started out well. The only thing he was lacking was a way to watch one of his favourite TV series. Kalani missed that, missed getting back into the characters' lives. Still, hopefully all this would blow over and he'd be back home soon.

What happened next showed him there'd be no chance of that.

The sun was rising, that crimson-gold glow climbing the skies like a boss, Kalani thought. Here, the sun owned the day and didn't let anyone forget it. He brewed himself some coffee and opened the packet of croissants he'd bought at the store yesterday, careful to stow away the plastic wrapper. The coffee was scalding, which was how he liked it, the croissants soft. He'd just finished up and was chucking his last dregs of coffee when he heard the approach of several men.

A bolt of horror shot through Kalani.

Was it Lynskey's crew? Or was it Tom Pierce and his new cohorts?

Kalani slipped into the brush. He knew how to blend in with the land. Twenty seconds passed. It was then that he remembered his bag and ran back for it, scooped it up and vanished back into his surroundings.

Men appeared seconds later. Kalani, low to the ground and completely still, recognised them instantly. The 42K. Nine of them. His blood froze. These men actually wanted to kill him, and nobody would bat an eyelid whilst one of them ran a razor-sharp blade across his throat. He felt as though he was in a TV series, the hard-done-by hunted protagonist.

The men came through, noisy and brash. Kalani felt shock at seeing the man who led them. Lynskey. The cop, one of three who secretly ran the 42K. They didn't think he knew, but Kalani was as shrewd as he was practical and always kept an ear and an eye out. Information came to him randomly, as if collected on the breeze. He listened, and he watched, and soon, he knew everything.

Why the hell had Lynskey come out to do the dirty work? Was it that important to him? Was it something to do with Kamehameha? It was risky, but then Kalani guessed Lynskey was far from home, in a quiet place. Maybe he thought the risk was worth the payoff.

Because the payoff would be huge.

Kalani stayed deathly still as the entourage passed. They were slowing as they went, perhaps believing they were reaching their destination. Kalani then felt surprise and trepidation to see a second group creeping through the forest after the first. His blood ran even colder. This was Tom Pierce and his crew, tracking the 42K.

Kalani could see exactly where this was going, and it wasn't anywhere good. He was about to be caught in the middle of a fight. *Dammit.* If he made a move now, they would surely hear or see him. If he stayed put, he risked getting caught in the middle of it or catching a stray bullet. Why couldn't they all just stay out of his business?

It was an impossible choice. Kalani decided flight was better than fight. If he could just slip backwards for a hundred yards or so, then run for it, he might just get clear before everything kicked off.

But he was too slow. The action began even before he'd moved ten yards. Bullets flew, some of them slamming into trees right above his head. Kalani flattened out, holding his hands over his head as if that'd help deflect anything stray that headed his way. There was shouting and general mayhem from the clearing.

Then it seemed as if the two warring parties were just concentrating on each other. Kalani saw his chance. He scrambled backwards, rose behind a wide tree, and took a deep breath. He had to force himself to calm down, to breathe, so he stood for a moment, back to the tree, and waited. The gunfire continued. Men screamed, and once, Kalani heard a knife slicing flesh. He was shocked at Pierce; the PI never got involved in this kind of thing, but then maybe he was doing it for Kalani.

Maybe he did care after all...

There was no time for reflection or even too much thought. Kalani needed to vanish into the foliage, never to be seen again. He couldn't see the battle and took a chance. He stepped out, prepared to race into the trees. There was a cry. Kalani looked back. One man had seen him and was giving chase. The man held a wicked-looking knife in his right hand. Kalani ignored the terror and ran, thundering between the trees, trying to find a trail. He leapt fallen branches, clambered over deadfalls and squeezed between wide trunks, heading deeper into the greenery. The sound of the man following him was loud, unmistakable, and it was coming closer.

The guy took chances, fell headlong twice, but survived without injury and kept coming. He was yelling, pinpointing his position, running as though he were invincible, hacking with the knife as he came and telling Kalani exactly what he was going to do to him. Kalani believed every word and ran, ran as he never had before.

But the guy was closing. He was recklessly fast. Kalani couldn't outpace him. He cut through the woodland, cutting left and right, but now the guy was just a hundred yards behind, and now, eighty, now fifty...

Kalani saw one chance. There was a long, sharp drop up ahead. He knew of it because he'd found it years ago and had almost fallen down it. The drop came up suddenly, and it was sheer. Kalani had to time it just right. He slowed a little, let the guy catch up a bit more, spurred him on by looking back with fear all over his face.

The guy's own face was grim, but happy. He knew he was going to catch Kalani. Maybe there was a reward out for him. Maybe the good graces of his boss – Lynskey – were all this guy needed.

Kalani slowed some more, saw the wide open gaps through the trees ahead that signalled no more forest, and ran through the last line. He swerved instantly, cutting left. The guy, a step behind, lunged and...

... well, he fell head first down a very long, very bumpy slope. His scream of shock and terror was abruptly cut off. He flew through the air at first, then landed hard on his chest and then started rolling. He rolled for an age, bouncing off rocks and trees and thick foliage, tearing himself up.

Kalani watched for a short while, then, seeing that the chase had put him quite a distance from the battle, took advantage of that. He circumvented the entire area, keeping the long drop at his back and weaving his way through the trees. He couldn't hear anything from here, did not know what was happening back there, but knew his way unerringly through the woodland and managed to get back to the other side in just a few brief hours.

From here, it was a relatively short trek back to Lihue.

But questions remained. How had they found him this time? How had they *all* found him? Was he really that predictable, that easy to find? Of course, Tom Pierce knew him well, but the 42K had barely bothered with him and he'd been happy with that.

Kauai was unsafe.

Kalani walked quickly into Lihue. As he approached, he took out his phone and called a number he barely used. When the call was answered, he spoke just a few short words.

'Halia,' he said. 'I need your help. Is the beach hut still free?'

CHAPTER SEVENTEEN

At first, Alicia didn't know which way to turn.

'Lynskey's a cop?' she repeated, staring at Pierce. 'Are you sure?'

'I know my cops,' Pierce grunted. 'And I've come across him a few times back on Oahu. Real piece of work.'

'But why would he be on Kauai, leading a gang of thieves and cutthroats?'

Pierce shrugged. 'Probably felt like he had to get involved. Kauai's more remote. We're in a very quiet area. Probably thought he'd be okay.'

Alicia tried to take it in. 'So, Lynskey's the leader of the 42K?'

'He's in the right place to protect them,' Crouch said.

'I didn't say he was the big boss,' Pierce said. 'I don't know. He could be a lackey to someone.'

They couldn't stand around here talking and Alicia knew it. She dropped the line of questioning. Kalani wasn't here. The surviving members of the 42K had already quit the area.

'We have to get out of here,' she said.

They quickly hiked back in the direction of Lihue. They speculated as to where Kalani had gone and where he might be now. It didn't help. Pierce made sure his phone was on loud and checked the charge. He told them he was expecting a call.

'About Kalani?' Caitlyn asked.

'I told you. I have eyes and ears everywhere, more than the 42K. Once Kalani arrives somewhere, we'll know.'

'And Kalani's problem is that he's well known across the islands,' Crouch said.

'Yeah, a fact that works both for and against him. I mean, we know where Kalani's going before he does.' Pierce laughed.

They headed back toward Lihue. For Alicia, it was an odd feeling. Essentially, they were directionless, hoping for help. It was far from what she was used to. But Pierce appeared to know what he was doing and seemed happy to rely on his network of contacts. For now, she would trust that he indeed knew what he was doing.

Caitlyn was engrossed in her phone as they drove. Alicia knew it would be purely professional, none of this social media crap for Caitlyn. Without asking, Alicia knew she'd be researching Kamehameha so that, when the time came, she'd be the informed one.

Russo sat like a grumpy mountain in one corner of the car, staring straight forward and on the edge of his seat as if waiting for a call to action. Crouch sat in the passenger seat, quietly conversing with Pierce, drawing forth as much information as he could. That was just like Crouch, she thought, trying to cover every angle and never failing to get the full picture.

Which left her.

Alicia knew it had been a close call back there. The 42K were a typical gang, not dazzling overall, made up of too many fools and not enough thinkers, but they were well armed and they had a sense of purpose. Alicia had been told they were numerous too, so there'd be no chance of them letting up just yet. Also, why had Lynskey got involved? She understood they were in a remote place here, but risk was risk. The cop could get desperate, which wasn't going to help anything.

Alicia reflected all the way back to Lihue, where they stopped for food and water and ate it in the car. The fare wasn't great, just pre-packed sandwiches, but it filled a hole. Nobody spoke much, just Pierce remarking on how quiet his phone was.

But they took a chance. They headed straight for the airport.

'How far behind him are we?' Caitlyn asked at one point.

'Could be hours,' Pierce said. 'Which would actually help in tracking him down. Kalani is stuck. He knows he has to keep moving. He won't stay in one place for long, not until he feels safe. And that means he must keep calling his friends.'

'The poor guy will be desperate,' Caitlyn sounded sorry for him.

'Don't forget he brought this on himself,' Russo said. 'Kalani was stealing from the criminals.'

'Oh, you're all heart,' Alicia said. 'He didn't want to be a part of this life. He fell into it. Maybe he was pushed. We've all done things we don't want to do to stay alive.'

Russo eyed her. 'What did you do?'

'Figure of speech,' Alicia said quickly. 'You know what I mean. And, yes, I was on the wrong side of the criminal tracks once.'

The car was nearing the airport, Pierce slowing down as they got stuck in traffic. The airport itself was small and unobtrusive, barely a blot on the landscape. Because he couldn't go anywhere yet, Pierce took his time.

'You're gonna look real stupid if he's stayed on Kauai,' Alicia said.

Pierce shrugged. 'Just doing my best here. My best for Kalani. I have a dozen other jobs I could be jumping on.'

'Missing cats?' Alicia smiled. 'Broken tennis rackets?'

'Something like that,' Pierce had to grin.

It was right then that his phone rang. Pierce pulled over at the side of the road, flicked his indicator on, and answered the phone. He listened for a while, then thanked the caller and hung up.

'I know where he went,' he said.

'Where?' Alicia asked.

'He's hightailed it to Molokai. Another island.'

'Why?' Crouch asked.

'I don't know. Maybe he feels safer there. But I know exactly where he's gone. He's staying in Halia's beach hut.'

'Let me guess. Halia told you that.' Alicia said.

'Yeah, she's an old friend. She knows I only have Kalani's best interests at heart. Halia is a good woman. She's looking out for the kid.'

'So where's this Molokai?' Russo asked.

'Not far. It's on the other side of Oahu.'

'Let me ask you this,' Crouch said, as Pierce pocketed his phone and slid back into the line of traffic. 'Will the 42K be fed the same information?'

'Not from Halia,' Pierce said. 'But if he's been seen by someone else, by all the watching eyes, then I can't rule it out.'

'A beach hut sounds remote,' Caitlyn said.

'It is,' Pierce nodded. 'But there's always the problem of supplies. Of arriving on the island and then reaching your destination. That's where you can mess it all up.'

'He'll have flown?' Crouch asked.

'Definitely. A boat would take too long.'

'Sounds to me like Kalani needs to stop flitting between islands,' Russo said.

Pierce raised an eyebrow at him. 'We're in Hawaii, brah,' he said. 'Where the hell else do you want him to go?'

It was a fair point. Alicia settled back as Pierce neared the airport and told them that flights between the islands were quite frequent.

'Let me guess,' Alicia said. 'You know someone who has space on a plane?'

'Not yet,' Pierce returned. 'But give me ten minutes.'

CHAPTER EIGHTEEN

Molokai, nicknamed *Aina Momona*, the Friendly Isle, is the fifth most populous of the eight major islands that form the Hawaiian Islands Archipelago. Its economy thrives from cattle ranching, pineapple production and farming, rather than tourism, which was mostly closed off in the early 2000's. Molokai boasts the highest sea cliffs in the world.

The plane banked and came in at an angle. Alicia held on tight, pulling her seatbelt closer around her body. It was a fast descent; the ground coming up quickly to meet the flimsy little plane. The pilot levelled out at the last minute, cut the speed, and then bounded down the runway, not catering for the comfort of his passengers, it seemed.

Soon they were in the heat of the day, walking with a few other people into the main terminal and winding their way through customs. The problem with island hopping was that they could never hang on to any weapons, Alicia mused as she waited in line. And she was grateful that Pierce knew his way around.

Soon, they were departing the airport in a hire car and headed for a nearby town. Pierce explained his thoughts as he drove.

'Kalani must be terrified,' he said. 'But not just that. He knows *why* the 42K are really chasing him. He knows it's all about Kamehameha. It's the greatest prize in history. We need to keep hold of him for the same reason, but for different purposes.'

'Kamehameha isn't going anywhere,' Russo said.

'But he will if the 42K gets to him first,' Pierce said. 'Shit, for all we know, they'll destroy him. We don't know *what* they'll do.'

Alicia thought that extreme, but she understood what Pierce was saying. They had a responsibility to save Kalani now for the Hawaiian people, for the entire culture. Nothing was more important to them than Kamehameha.

Pierce drove them to a small town where he set about hiring a boat. He explained to them that the fastest way to reach Kalani was directly across the water. They could go straight to the place where the beach hut was situated without having to drive around the roads.

'Point to point, it's quicker,' he told them.

'I'm not big on boats,' Russo said.

'Suck it up, big boy,' Alicia told him.

Russo gave her the eye. Pierce interrupted them by saying, 'Don't worry, we're not talking about a dinghy here. We're looking for something larger.'

They found a rental place by the beach where a wide dock jutted out into the sea. As Pierce had already told them, there weren't many tourists about. Molokai didn't cater for them. These boats would be rented to locals for day jaunts or weekly holidays or any number of reasons. Pierce, being a native, ought to have no problem renting a boat.

What he came up with made Alicia nod in satisfaction. It was an eight-person powerboat with a hardtop, a cabin cruiser. Pierce clambered aboard after he'd signed the papers and set about being captain, making sure all was well before starting the engines. Alicia wasn't sure whether to sit or stand, but made do with leaning against a bulkhead as Pierce pulled away from the jetty. The two men who'd rented them the boat gave them a wave and then they were plying through the sparkling blue seas off the coast of Molokai.

The sun beat down from overhead. Alicia hid under her hat and slapped a load of suntan lotion on. Pierce used his phone to navigate, trying to pinpoint the beach hut and then plot a straight, arrow-like course to it across the waves without venturing too far out from shore. The coastline of Molokai spread out to their left, the islands distinct extinct volcanoes rising above. Alicia saw a lot of trees and rolling hills and greenery and more than a few homesteads as they skipped through the waves.

The surf soared into the air as the boat's brow slipped through the dazzling waters. Alicia slid some sunglasses on. She plucked a bottle of water from her rucksack and drank deeply. The wind generated by the speed of the boat felt good on her skin. Around her, the team lounged, catching a rest before they reached the beach hut and might be called into action again.

Pierce piloted the boat with ease. Of course, living on the islands, he'd done this before, driven between numerous places just for the fun of it. He stayed silent though, his face impassive as though worry and guilt and nervous anticipation were all weighing him down. He didn't look at them but followed the route he'd plotted on his phone, the route that would take them directly to Kalani's beach hut.

Time passed. Alicia wondered if the 42K would come by the same information that they had. If they did, she had to be ready for a firefight and, once again, she had no weapons other than her hands and fists.

Steadily, they skipped around the island and saw a white, sandy beach ahead. Pierce aimed for it. The beach was shaped like a horseshoe and wide, running up to a treeline through which ran many gaps, the trees drooping and parched there, hanging as if they had just about had enough.

'The beach hut is up there?' Alicia asked.

'Beyond the treeline,' Pierce said tightly.

Alicia noticed how uptight he seemed. 'Do you know something we don't?'

Pierce bit his lower lip. 'I'm eager to find Kalani, that's all. I'm anxious to get to Kamehameha before the 42K do. Anxious not to meet them again. Our luck will only stretch so far.'

'You think we were lucky back on Kauai?'

Pierce shrugged. 'Luck is dodging or catching a stray bullet. Doesn't matter how good or bad you are, it all comes down to being in the wrong place at the right time.'

'I don't agree,' Alicia said. 'It comes down to the skill of the operative. You can't underestimate ability.'

Pierce didn't answer. He was too busy guiding them to a certain spot along the shoreline. Alicia felt the wind rush lessen as the boat slowed, and a heating of her limbs. Pierce deployed the anchor rather than grounding them and then looked towards the beach.

'Let's go,' he said.

They leapt overboard, landing in the warm, clear waters with a splash. They slogged to the beach and then stood on the smooth white sand. Alicia looked at Pierce.

'How far?'

'Not far at all. You can see the beach hut from here.'

Alicia blinked, narrowed her eyes and looked to where he was pointing. There was no easy way to sneak up on the squat, square structure, which might have been one reason Kalani chose it. Trees marched up and down its sides, but the front area was wide open, just a door and a window.

Pierce stood in full view and waved his arms.

'Kalani!' he yelled. 'It's me! Again!'

Alicia winced at the noise, but knew there was no alternative. Kalani wouldn't be dumb enough not to be keeping a lookout, and there was no way they could approach the hut without being seen. Pierce's best option was to go loud.

'You there?' he yelled. 'Kalani, it's me!'

It was then that Alicia became aware of a presence in the trees. Someone was watching them from not too far away, someone who had been there a while and had just decided to make himself known.

Kalani.

The young man stepped out into the open and spread his arms. 'Tom,' he said. 'What the hell are you doing here, brah? You followed me from Oahu and Kauai?'

Pierce turned towards the youth. 'Here to help, buddy. You can't do this alone.'

'I told you. I don't need your help. I can do this myself. I *have* to do it myself. The 42K are all over it.'

'We know,' Alicia said. 'We took a few of them out on the other island.'

Kalani took a few steps towards them. A good sign. 'I saw,' he said. 'But what do you want from me?'

It was a testing question. He was probing their motives because he didn't believe they would be more interested in him than the treasure. He'd aimed his question at Michael Crouch, who, maybe, he saw as their leader.

'We want to protect you,' Crouch told him. 'We've said it before. The best way to do that is to find Kamehameha and get it all out in the open. You can't continue to run and hide and carry this burden around with you.'

'It won't work, brah,' Pierce said.

Kalani pursed his lips. 'Nobody ever offered to help me before,' he said. 'I don't even know if I can trust you.'

'Do you trust me?' Pierce asked.

Kalani eyed him. 'Maybe,' he said.

It was better than nothing, Alicia decided. She glanced at Russo and nodded back at the beach and the surrounding area. The big guy huffed and turned around, happy to be a lookout. He scanned the glittering seas first, and the span of the beach and then started around towards the beach hut where he would get the lie of the land. Alicia kept her eyes between Kalani and the sea.

'You want to join forces?' Kalani asked.

'That's exactly what we want. Together, we're stronger,' Pierce closed the gap between himself and Kalani.

'Last time, you brought the bad guys with you.'

Pierce made a face. 'My friend,' he said. 'They were already on your trail. If I can track you, they can track you. And they have far heavier options than I do. Coercion. Violence. You know how it goes.'

Kalani blinked. 'You're saying I'm not safe here?' He looked like a deer caught in the headlights.

Pierce held out a placating hand. 'You're not safe anywhere. That's why we're chasing you. Kalani, if you don't let us help, they will catch you.'

Now, Kalani looked scared. That people kept tracking him down couldn't be lost on him. However hard he tried, he was always on somebody's radar. 'You think they're coming to Molokai?' he asked.

Alicia raised a hand to shield her eyes. 'I think they're already here,' she said.

It wasn't a mirage on the horizon. Looking across the waves, she could see several boats approaching. They came skimming across the waters at top speed and, as they came closer, she could see a large group of men inside.

'Three boats,' she said. 'After what happened last time, they're gonna be ready.'

'Shit,' Pierce said. 'Kalani, do you have any weapons in the hut?'

They all looked around.

Kalani was gone.

CHAPTER NINETEEN

'Shit,' Pierce yelled.

Russo came back around the side of the hut, rushing towards them. 'What's wrong?'

Alicia pointed at the incoming boats. 'Company,' she said.

Russo didn't hang around. He ran, with Pierce, to the hut and kicked in the door. Alicia remained on the beach, watching along with Crouch and Caitlyn. The boats were small dinghies, approaching fast. They didn't have much more than five minutes. Alicia ran scenarios through her mind, wondering what was the best thing to do.

Seconds ticked by. Russo and Pierce came out of the hut, practically empty-handed. They held knives in their hands and passed one to Alicia. She turned back to the ocean and squinted.

'You think we should run?' Caitlyn asked.

'I'm ready to kick arse,' Alicia said.

'They're gonna start shooting soon,' came a fresh voice. Alicia turned to see Kalani now standing by them.

'Shit, kid,' she said. 'I thought you'd done another runner.'

'I did, but I came back.'

'Thank you,' Pierce said gratefully. 'I'm happy that you trust me.'

'Like you said – there's no choice.'

'Okay. Well, that doesn't please me as much as what you said before, but I'll take it.'

By now, the approaching boats were closing in fast. They were spread out, sizeable gaps between the three, but all zoning in on the same point. Alicia looked around at her companions.

'Ready?' she asked.

'They'll kill us,' Caitlyn said.

'Who wants to live forever?'

Alicia was only ever going to approach this scenario one way. Attack. She wouldn't stand idly by as a horde of enemies came at her. She had to engage them, to upset them, confront them. Now, she raced across the beach and dashed into the waters, holding her knife steady. She ran through the shallows, splashing hard. When she saw the rifles raised, she dived under the waves, pulling hard. She lifted her head, heard the report of gunshots. But the boats were closing in fast; she was almost upon them.

She sensed Russo at her side, the big man lumbering along with her, crouching in the surf as a bullet flew between them. Back on the beach, Caitlyn and Kalani had retreated to the relative safety of the trees, whilst Crouch had hidden behind a stray rock formation, head poking out.

The boats slowed as they approached the beach. Alicia rose from the waves, shedding water, and tackled the nearest man to her, grabbed him under the arms and hauled him out of the boat. He came easily, head first, and landed with a splutter. She fell to her knees, dunking her head under the water, and delivered a thrust to his chest. The knife sank in to the hilt. She pulled it out again and reached for the weapon he'd dropped.

A fully loaded Glock.

There was gunfire around her now, men jumping into the shallows. Boots landed to left and right. Alicia struck out, catching them, then ducking under bodies as men leaned out of the boat, guns in hand. She counted six men to each boat, which put her and Russo at a serious disadvantage.

But Russo was going crazy. Alicia had seen the rage take him before, turning him into a berserker, a madman who saw nothing but red. But this wasn't that. This was controlled rage, precise and skilful. Yelling out, he ducked under the prow of the nearest boat, rose up and tilted it sideways, upsetting the balance of everyone on board. Some men fell out, others rolled around the bottom, losing their grips on their weapons.

Russo splashed across to the next boat and did the same. Alicia saw men all around her, wallowing and wading in the waters, and brought the Glock up.

She opened fire. Men fell backwards. The waves kept coming, spattering her face as she tried to stand her ground. She reached out, grabbed the boat, and hauled herself aboard. There were more weapons here, and she reached out to grab herself a few before the 42K could recover from the onslaught. She emptied her Glock and then started using a new one.

A man came at her wielding a machete. Alicia, gun in hand, didn't have time to use it. Instead, she let herself fall backward off the boat so that the machete scythed thin air, passing inches from her head as she hit the waves. She went under, aimed the Glock through the waters and fired. Machete man fell backwards and disappeared.

Russo was still heaving the other boats. Men were falling overboard and crawling around the bottom. He'd scooped up a handgun and a rifle by now, and had slung the rifle over his shoulder. It was a tad unwieldy in the close quarter combat.

Just then, Alicia saw the rush of water and then Crouch appeared at her side. He threw out a couple of elbows, knocked men off their feet. He came to her side, reaching, and she gave him a handgun, which he then turned on two attackers.

They fell back, bleeding into the water.

Alicia stood upright, assessing the situation.

Men floated all around, most of them face down. A few were on the boat, just getting to their knees. Another just launched himself into the water, into the middle of the melee, unarmed, punching out like a madman. To Alicia's right, the third boat had passed her by and was now grinding up onto the beach; its contingent of men jumping out onto the sand. Russo had a man around the neck and was choking him out.

Crouch span to her. 'Go,' he said. 'We have to protect Caitlyn and Kalani.'

Alicia found herself dashing once more through the shallows. She reached the boat as its occupants were just climbing out, aimed her handgun and fired. She caught three of them with three quick shots, the reports so fast they almost sounded like one. Next, she raced around the boat and smashed another man across the back of the head.

By now, they were all turning towards her. She counted three more. So far, she hadn't seen Lynskey. It occurred to her then that she hadn't seen Pierce, either. Was he hiding with Caitlyn and Kalani? It didn't seem like him, but then she hardly knew him.

Pierce had told them he was ex-military.

And suddenly, he was there, helping out. He ran towards the front of the boat, taking the attention of the three men, threw a knife and saw it clatter off one man harmlessly. He came in low, sliding across the sand as they took aim at him.

Perfect, Alicia thought. Pierce had distracted them.

She fired three shots, heard the gun go empty. The men staggered and fell and died. But now there were more men splashing in from the ocean, having clambered out of the boats and waded through the shallows.

Alicia ran to the boats, reached up and grabbed the men remaining before they could climb out. They splashed headfirst into rolling water, disoriented and waving their arms around. Alicia smashed them across the top of the head with her empty weapon, kicked them in the face, kneed two others. A man raised a gun, taking aim at her. Alicia fought on. Russo smashed an elbow into the man's back, sending him sprawling, making him lose his grip on the gun.

It was a crazy melee. Pierce fought three men on the beach. Many floated in the clear waters. Alicia pulled two more men off their boats and deposited them in the ocean. Crouch had taken a nasty knock to the head and was kneeling in the shallows.

Both Caitlyn and Kalani were visible close to the treeline.

Alicia headed back to the beach as their attackers tried to leave the water.

Caitlyn held on to Kalani, not for protection but to stop him from running. 'We have control of this,' she said.

'It sure doesn't look that way.'

'The 42K outnumbers us, yes, but we're far better fighters. Look at Alicia and Rob. Do they look as if they're gonna lose?'

Kalani swallowed hard. 'I get all my action fix from the TV. NCIS, that kind of thing. I don't do it in real life. It's too much.'

'It is a tad more visceral,' Caitlyn admitted. 'And I won't say you get used to it, because you don't. But Kalani, this is where you stand with us.'

Kalani observed the battle, looking like he wanted to bolt. If he did, Caitlyn wouldn't be able to hold on to him. She sought a way to calm him down.

'What of Kamehameha?' she asked. 'You found something that's been missing for centuries. How did you do that?'

'I always wondered what was at the bottom of some particular steps,' Kalani told her. 'Very dangerous. You go right down towards a cliff drop. Follow the stairs. It feels like you're falling. Nothing in front of you and you can see right down to the rocks below. One day,' he shrugged. 'I just did it.'

'Courageous,' Caitlyn said.

'Just stupid, really,' Kalani said. 'I'm not known for my bright decisions.'

Caitlyn indicted the 42K. 'Like these guys?'

'Yeah, exactly like these guys.'

Caitlyn caught her breath as the battle moved towards them.

CHAPTER TWENTY

Kalani couldn't stand it any longer.

This was all too much for him. The enemy was closer than he could deal with. They wanted to kill him, and here they were running up the beach. Kalani was in plain sight. His heart hammered. Sweat stood out along his forehead and his mouth was bone dry. He couldn't just stand here and let them grab him.

But the woman, Caitlyn, was at his side. The others, Alicia, Russo, Crouch and Pierce, were all fighting hard. In fact, it looked as though they were winning. The 42K were lying everywhere, some bodies floating, some groaning, a few men screaming in pain. This wasn't like one of Kalani's favourite programmes – not when actual fear and adrenalin were racing hard through his system. He wanted to stay, needed to trust someone, to share his secret with them. He trusted Tom Pierce, had to assume that these other people were as good as the PI.

Am I leading the 42K to me every time?

What was he doing wrong? So far, they'd found him every time, and they were scarily accurate. Kalani thought he was only using a network of friends to flit from place to place, but what if that network was compromised?

Where else could he go?

There was one place.

It cheered Kalani up to think of it. But he couldn't get there alone. He'd need help. Which, again, brought the whole compromise thing into play.

The battle was ebbing closer. Kalani could hear the grunts of the attackers, the yells of his defenders. He saw Alicia grab hold of a man by his long hair, wrench his head back, and break his neck. He saw Russo land an elbow on a man, using his great bulk, and drive that man beneath the incoming waves. The man didn't get up again. He saw Tom Pierce on the beach, struggling with three men but using debilitating blows that he'd clearly learned in the military to remain on top. And the other guy, Crouch, he was acquitting himself well in the shallows.

The dinghies that the 42K had arrived in bobbed harmlessly amid the waves. They were empty now, one floating away.

Kalani clenched a fist in frustration. This was all about one thing. Essentially, it was about money but, on the surface, it was his knowledge of the whereabouts of King Kamehameha. All this bloodshed, these broken bones, all part of a foolish quest for a slice of history. How many foolish quests, just like this, had ended in death and destruction?

Kalani knew what he had to do.

He waited for his chance.

The battle drew closer still. Caitlyn and he walked back among the trees. Already, Kalani had seen two attackers recognise him. Alicia had taken care of both of them, but that wasn't the point. He felt too exposed standing out in the open like this.

It was time to go.

But how to get away from Caitlyn? He took a few steps back, so that he was on her blind side. He watched the battle. Every time one of the enemy started towards them, Caitlyn tensed with concern. Kalani watched her closely. When her concentration was fully on the battle, Kalani turned and slipped away.

He moved quietly and swiftly. The trees were thin at first, just saplings really, and he had to avoid lots of fallen branches and twigs. He made his way through the trees as the fighting got louder behind him.

Kalani felt better with every passing second. This was the right thing to do. Avoid the confrontation, slip away, always the best course of action when dealing with criminals. He slid through the trees, trying not to trip.

He didn't see the two heavy bulks until it was too late. Somehow, two members of the 42K had entered the treeline from the beach and were making their way through the foliage, probably hoping to come up behind Pierce and his team. Kalani saw them, stopped, and then tried to let out a yell of warning.

They didn't let him. They lunged at him, striking his chest and sending him staggering backwards. He fell, got to his knees, looked up at them.

'No,' he said.

They didn't listen. They threw their punches, knocking him to the ground, lined up in front of him with their boots.

'Kalani,' one of them said. 'We're gonna fuck you up, and then you're gonna tell us everything we want to know.'

'No,' he said again.

A boot slammed into his stomach, folding him. 'Oh, yeah,' one said. 'And, brah, I'm gonna enjoy this.'

Kalani struggled away, sliding backwards. The men followed at their leisure, laughing, making him wait for it.

'Where's the treasure?' one of them asked and then lashed out with his boots. Kalani dodged sideways, but slammed his face into a tree.

More laughter, one man choking with it. Another boot lashing, this one connecting with Kalani's right knee. He couldn't help but scream as the pain lanced through him. He was sitting upright, looking up at them.

'You're crazy if you think I'll tell you anything.'

'Good,' the man on the left said. 'That means we get to beat you harder.'

Kalani tried to rise, but the pain in his knee was too much. He staggered; they grinned. They caught him and threw him back against a tree. They punched him hard in the stomach, doubling him over. Kalani saw stars; he could barely breathe.

'Wait until we get everyone involved,' someone said. 'Now, that's gonna be fun.'

'He can run the gauntlet,' the other man guffawed.

And suddenly there was a fresh voice in the mix, a very welcome voice to Kalani's ears.

'What gauntlet?' Alicia's voice asked. 'Are you boys really beating on a man who won't hit you back?'

And she flew at them through the trees. She jabbed the first in the throat, then kicked out at his knee. When he grunted and lurched away, she turned to the second, blocked two of his punches and then clattered him over the head. He went down as if he'd been hammered into the ground, falling like a sack of rocks.

Alicia followed up with swift downward punches to both men, targeting the back of their necks and then their throats. She jabbed at one man's eyes, making him cry out. They fell, now squirming among the fallen branches as Kalani had been, holding their arms in the air to ward off their assailant.

Kalani saw his chance.

With the men and Alicia otherwise engaged, he ignored the pain in his knee and lurched away to the left, running through the trees. He didn't know in which direction he ran, but was confident he'd know where he was headed when he got there.

Alicia had saved him, but now Kalani had to save himself.

He raced away from the scene, putting on more speed as the pain in his knee subsided. Where would he end up? Were there more men waiting for him?

Kalani would take the chance. He was nothing if not tenacious in his escape. And it wasn't as though he was short of places to go.

Kalani fled.

CHAPTER TWENTY ONE

Alicia concentrated on defeating her two opponents and, by the time she looked up, Kalani had gone. *That kid,* she thought, *really should start trusting us.*

She left the two men unconscious in the undergrowth, thought about following Kalani, but knew her friends were still fighting back at the beach. She couldn't just leave them and go racing after one man. Alicia was about to turn back when she got quite a surprise.

Figures pushed their way through the trees. She recognised her team, led by Crouch.

'You running away from the fight?' Russo grunted at her.

'Saving Kalani,' she said.

'Huh,' the big man grumbled.

'How are you guys all here?' Alicia asked.

'We finished them off,' Pierce said with a shrug. 'But we'd better get a move on, because some of them will come around quite quickly.'

They'd left dead and unconscious men at the beach, Alicia knew. But now she saw the opportunity to go after Kalani.

'Let's go,' she said.

They moved rapidly, running through the sparse trees, trying to stay on Kalani's trail. Alicia vaulted ditches and squeezed between trunks, ducking underneath low-hanging boughs. She caught her ankle on a fallen branch and stumbled headlong, lucky that she didn't pitch forward and injure herself. After that, they slowed down a little.

But the chase for Kalani continued. They rushed through the stand of trees, pushing through the thick of it at the centre, and then reaching the far side where the trees became sparser, thinner, and weaker.

They burst out into the open. They were far on the other side of the beach hut now, but they could look back at it. They heard the roar of an engine, saw a small black truck start to move. It came towards them, veered aside, and passed them by at speed. Alicia saw Kalani in the driver's seat.

He didn't look at them.

'Stop!' Pierce was yelling, gesturing at the truck as it sped by. 'We can help you!'

'There's gonna be no stopping him,' Crouch said. 'Kalani's already on another mission.'

'We saved his ass,' Alicia muttered.

'But did we also bring the 42K down on him?' Caitlyn asked, shielding her eyes as she watched the truck drive away.

'No, he did that to himself,' Pierce said. 'By using his so-called friends' network. And he'll continue to use it. Kalani is too trusting.'

Alicia shook her head. 'He doesn't look like it right now.'

'I meant with the people he sees as friends. If I was going after him alone, he'd probably trust me.'

'He's an idiot,' Alicia said.

'Oh, agreed. A first-class fool. But that will not help us find him.'

'Where do you think he'll go?'

'Another island, I guess. The problem is, he's running out of them.'

If Pierce was attempting to create a light-hearted moment, it didn't work. Alicia was pissed that Kalani kept running away from them, pissed that this so-called treasure hunt had stalled before it even began, pissed that the 42K kept on finding them. Did Kalani even deserve their help?

'We could end it right here,' she said. 'Kalani obviously doesn't want our help.'

'You always were the headstrong one,' Crouch came up to her. 'Look at it through his eyes. He's shit scared. On the run. Doesn't know which way to turn except to the channels he knows so well. Does he know those channels are compromised? Maybe, maybe not. But it's all he's ever known. It's what he trusts, not some out-of-towners. To him, we're no better than tourists.'

Alicia snorted. 'I think that's the first time anyone's ever called me a tourist.'

By now, the truck was practically out of sight as it joined a main road hundreds of yards distant. Pierce already had his phone out.

'Who are you calling?' Caitlyn asked.

Pierce turned to them and said, predictably, 'A friend.'

'Does your friend know how to drive?' Alicia asked, staring left and right, knowing they couldn't go back to their boat, and understanding their new predicament.

Pierce nodded. They sent Russo back up the track just in case the 42K investigated further and then walked on to the road, taking cover there. Russo came back shortly and reported that the 42K ransacked the beach hut but did little else. They were as angry as

Alicia, on the phone to their bosses and taking the brunt of their fury.

Less than an hour later, a truck with a flatbed turned up. Alicia found herself climbing into the back and hanging on. Russo joined her. Everyone else travelled up front. The truck took off at speed, slewing gravel from under its tyres. The driver left the sliding glass panel at the back of the cab open so that Alicia and Russo could hear their conversation.

'Where to?' he asked Pierce.

'Somewhere important,' Caitlyn said. 'We may have to head off quickly to another island.'

The driver laughed softly. 'There are no cities on Molokai,' he said with a smile at her. 'No large malls or stores. Not even a traffic light. We don't have a capital here, it is all the state of Maui. What we have are sleepy little towns and villages.'

Caitlyn looked surprised. Pierce nodded.

'The chief town is Kaunakakai. Take us there, my friend.'

'Sure.'

They hunkered down for their trip. Alicia saw low hills and stands of trees and brown fields as they hammered down the road. She saw the odd rural farmstead, a few small villages here and there. Their driver managed their expectations about Kaunakakai, explaining that it was just three city blocks in size and that the majority of the stores and eateries were located on Ala Malama Avenue and that most of the buildings they would see were of original construction.

It was getting dark. Alicia wondered what the hell they were going to do about the oncoming night. Were there any hotels? She voiced her concerns.

'Hotel Molokai is just five minutes from Kaunakakai. It's located on Kamiloloa beach, near Hawaii's only barrier reef. A fabulous place. They say Aloha is a way of life there.'

Alicia listened in relief, but then blinked as Pierce spoke up.

'But we're not staying there,' he said.

'We're getting straight off the island?' Crouch asked. 'But how can we do that if we don't yet know where Kalani has gone?'

'We can't leave yet,' Pierce said. 'You are right. We have to wait for word of Kalani to filter through. We're staying with my friend Alakai, here,'

Alicia frowned. 'All of us?'

'Yeah, it'll be cramped, but we can all bunk in, right?'

Alicia gave Russo a heavy lidded look. 'No way am I bunking in with you, man.'

'And I wouldn't risk sleeping next to you.'

'What's that supposed to mean?'

'You'd be trying to jump my bones all night.'

'Oh, do you think I'm that desperate?'

'Every damn day.'

Alicia wondered if a punch to the nose might make her feel better about Russo. It certainly couldn't hurt. She was still trying to decide when their driver, Alakai, swung into a dirt driveway and down a rutted track. Now, it was all Alicia could do to hang on and remain in place rather than being bumped right out of the truck.

Alakai pulled up. A dust cloud swirled around the truck, and the engine ticked in the sudden silence. Alicia saw a rambling farmhouse, a large barn, and several other outbuildings. She turned quickly to Russo.

'I see your place,' she said. 'The barn...'

'Not a chance.'

'No, I was thinking of the kennels right in front.'

Russo ignored her and jumped off the back of the truck. As he did, several dogs came bounding up to them, barking in excitement. Russo looked wary. Alicia stayed right in the back of the truck. Alakai opened his door and whistled at the dogs, calling them off. Then everyone exited the truck.

Alicia was shown to a small bedroom with a single bed, a curtained window and not much else. But she'd been in far worse. After they'd showered and changed, Alakai put on a traditional Hawaiian soup and a stew and invited everyone to sit at his long table in the cluttered kitchen. Pierce sat with his phone in front of him, just waiting for the next call.

It was a long night. After the stew came an iconic Hawaiian dessert, what Alakai called *Malassadas,* essentially Hawaii's version of doughnuts, like brioche but softer, deep-fried and rolled in sugar and then filled with tasty ingredients.

Alicia ate until she was more than full, constantly flicking her attention to Pierce's phone. He received quite a few messages and calls, but none of them involved Kalani. Of course, Pierce had an ongoing business on Oahu and had left it in the hands of a couple of capable friends.

Still later, Alakai brought out the spiced rum.

It was always Alicia's favourite and, since they had time to kill, she thought it entirely responsible to partake.

'Robster?' she asked Russo. 'Can you handle a drop of rum?'

'You're just trying to get me drunk.'

'I'm sure it won't take much.'

Russo held his glass out. Alicia filled it to the top. She filled her own up too, then clinked glasses with Russo, and knocked the shot back. Around the table, everyone drank and soon the bottle was empty.

Alakai produced another bottle.

Alicia could see this was headed towards a messy night. She didn't care. They'd been fighting and chasing their own tails for a long time – or at least it felt like a long time – and she was sick of Kalani's constant running. She knocked back shot after shot, allowing the alcohol to take off the edge. Even Caitlyn let her hair down.

Alicia did not know what time it was when she went to bed. She didn't care. She was happy for the first time since she'd arrived in Hawaii. Kalani would be found or he would not be, and the same stood for Kamehameha.

To hell with them all.

CHAPTER TWENTY TWO

The next morning, she wasn't so carefree.

Her head certainly hurt, and her mouth was dry. She woke up to see Tom Pierce standing over her.

'What the fuck are you doing in my room?'

'Making sure you're alive. I was thinking of dragging you out of bed.'

'Do it, pal, and you'll lose an arm. At least.'

Pierce grinned, none the worse for wear after his night of drinking. 'That might be worth the risk.'

Alicia blinked up at him. Was the guy flirting with her? To be fair, she was an aggressive, confident woman, not the kind of figure men flirted with and hoped to get away with it. She'd pretty much forgotten the art of flirting. It wasn't really in her nature. Alicia said what she meant, straight out, and to hell with anyone who didn't like it.

She stared up at Pierce now. 'Are you still here?'

'Still contemplating.'

'Go contemplate somewhere else. I need to get up and get dressed.'

'Breakfast in five minutes.'

'Wait,' Alicia said as Pierce turned to leave the room. 'Have you heard anything about Kalani?'

'That's the reason for the rude interruption,' Pierce said. 'Get dressed.'

Ten minutes and a forty-five second shower later, Alicia was walking into the kitchen where Alakai had laid out a few plates of pastries and made a large pot of fresh coffee. Alicia helped herself with a grateful nod to their host. Around the table, the others already sat munching their breakfast.

'So,' Pierce said once Alicia had seated herself. 'I've received intel from a friend that Kalani has landed on Lanai.'

Alicia didn't recognise the name. 'Lanai. Is that another island?'

'He's definitely doing the rounds,' Crouch said.

'Lanai is the smallest publicly accessible island in the chain,' Pierce said. 'With only one town of note, that's the imaginatively titled Lanai City. It's known locally as the Pineapple Island because once it was an island-wide pineapple plantation.'

'And Kalani has gone there now?' Alicia asked. 'Doesn't he see that the less inhabited the island is, the easier it is to find him?'

'He's on the run,' Pierce said. 'Being chased by killers. People don't think too clearly in that situation.'

Alicia inclined her head, accepting that. From what she had heard and seen of Kalani, the guy seemed like a normal civilian and, to be fair, civilians were pretty predictable. They mostly thought the same way. And a lot of it had to do with the shows they watched on television.

'Do you know where on Lanai?' Caitlyn asked.

Pierce laughed at that. 'You won't believe it after what I just said, but he's hiding out in an old pineapple plantation.'

Alicia closed her eyes, fearing for the kid. 'This time, we can't slip up,' she said. 'We have to save him.'

'Are you ready to go?' Pierce asked.

Alicia nodded. 'Just point me in the right direction.'

They moved out. Alakai drove them to Kaunakakai, where they rented a fast motorboat. Luckily, Lanai was right next to Molokai, just a quick hop and a skip across the waves. Alicia was inside their rental boat, backpack fastened tightly, standing and holding on to a support by the time Pierce was ready to set off.

It was relatively early, about 8.30 a.m. The rising sun was already heating the day, a fresh breeze skimming across the surface of the ocean. It was bright enough to need sunglasses and sun cream and all the other inconvenient things you had to think about in a tropical paradise, especially if you were blonde and fair skinned like Alicia. She wandered over to Caitlyn as Pierce started up the boat.

'I guess you've been doing your research?'

'Oh dear, yes. If you want to know something about Kamehameha, just ask.'

'I'll pass, thanks.'

'He's fascinating as a historical figure. Do you know what mana is?'

Alicia winced, sensing a lecture coming on, but knew it was in Caitlyn's nature to be interested in the historical side of things. '

'Something to do with nature,' Alicia said vaguely.

'Even today, the Hawaiians place a good deal of importance on mana. It is the powerful energy of their spiritual nature. In the old days, mana was jealously guarded and increased day by day, week by week. The more mana you could accumulate, the more powerful you became. King Kamehameha was believed to have attained an immense amount of mana for several reasons. One, he was born at a time of storms and strange lights in the sky. Now mana relates to a force of nature, so storms and thunder and lightning are considered a good sign at birth. Two, he'd been well trained and grew up to be a strong, fierce warrior. Success in battle afforded you an abundance of mana. And, of course, he fought in the famous battle of Kealakekua Bay where Captain Cook was killed.'

Caitlyn continued to speak, but by now Pierce was heading out of the bay into the much choppier ocean. The wind blasted past them. Alicia hung on to the bulkhead, turning her attention from Caitlyn to the rolling waves. Spray flew up and coated her face. She'd imagined that a quick trip between the islands would be kind of pleasant. As it turned out, the waters between Molokai and Lanai were, today at least, rather rough.

Alicia held on. Caitlyn grasped a side rail behind her, looking green. The boat dipped in the troughs and rode high over the swells, already closing in on Lanai. Alicia guessed they were about thirty minutes from the new island. She took a moment to check on her other companions.

Pierce was driving, hanging on to the wheel. Crouch had belted himself into a passenger seat, a sensible man. Russo was standing on the other side of the boat, like Alicia, hanging on to one of the bulkhead supports. The big man looked about as green as she felt. When he caught her looking at him, he shook his head as if to say, *not now*. He clearly wasn't in the mood for a bit of teasing.

Alicia shouted over at him, 'What's the matter, Rob? Feeling ropey? Can't get your banter up?'

Russo gave her the finger. Alicia managed a laugh and felt a little better. She turned to Caitlyn.

'You were saying?'

'Never mind.'

The shores of Lanai grew larger and larger. It was then that Alicia became aware of another presence in the water.

'Oh, shit.'

Crouch turned around in his seat, catching the tone in her voice. 'I don't like the look of that,' he said.

Coming up behind them in two far more powerful boats, skimming across the waves, was a large contingent of men. Alicia could see them hanging off their boat and clustered in the cabin and in the back; she could also see some of the weapons they were carrying. Nobody seemed to be bothered about concealing their guns and other implements, and they were heading straight for Lanai. Alicia stared from face to face whilst, at the same time, trying not to appear too interested. She recognised none of them, but then, she'd only ever seen them in the heat of battle.

'Is that the 42K?' Russo asked.

Of course, it might not be the gang. Alicia knew there were other criminals that operated in Hawaii. But from the way they were speeding towards Lanai, to their body language, to the way they were dressed, told her they were the 42K. And there was a terrible feeling deep down in her gut, too.

Pierce glanced back as he drove.

'Do you recognise any of them?' Alicia asked.

'Unfortunately, I do,' Pierce said grimly. 'Several, in fact. This is not good.'

He poured on the speed, making the motorboat skim faster across the surface of the water, but the other boats were far more powerful, still gaining quickly on them, their white surfaces reflecting the sunlight.

They closed the gap.

'You think they recognise us?' Caitlyn asked.

'Doesn't matter if they do,' Alicia replied. 'We can't let them reach Lanai before we do. Not if we hope to keep Kalani safe.'

They'd held on to some of the weapons they'd confiscated back on Molokai, and now Alicia took hers from her rucksack. It was a Sig Sauer and had exactly eight bullets left in the mag. She checked it now, taking out the mag and trying the action. As she did so, the others tested their own weapons.

'Anyone have a plan?' Pierce yelled.

Alicia watched the advancing boats, unsure if they were threatening or just aiming to blast past. Surely if they just wanted to go through, they wouldn't all be holding their weapons in clear view, but then... .they were gang members. Who knew what was going on in their heads?

'Sit down,' Alicia said quietly. 'Keep your weapons well out of sight. Maybe if they get past us without incident, we can try to shoot out their engines and leave them dead in the water.'

Her shouted words just reached the ears of Pierce and Crouch, who both nodded with grim determination. The two speedboats drew closer. Alicia sat with her hands down past her knees, the others following suit. Pierce steered the boat steadily, his gun nestled in a little glove-box under the wheel. They kept the pace up; the boat bouncing across the chop. Lanai and its shores grew closer.

Alicia waited, glancing carefully at the oncoming boats. They did not alter their route and were aiming to pass close by. So close, in fact, that no matter what happened, the smaller boat would be caught violently in the chop of their wake.

Alicia readied herself. The sun beat down hard now, spray still misting up before her eyes. The two boats came closer and were now almost alongside. Alicia turned slightly to look at them.

And that was when they opened fire.

CHAPTER TWENTY THREE

Bullets peppered the side of their boat, glancing off and puncturing the glass-fibre hull.

Alicia dropped to her stomach, falling into the seawater that was swilling around the bottom of the boat.

'I think they recognise us!' she yelled.

'Maybe,' Russo wiggled a hand. 'Be better if you stick your head up and ask them.'

Bullets laced the air, the constant sound of them striking the boat with a staccato *rat-a-tat*. Pierce was ducking as best he could whilst still steering the boat. Crouch had unbuckled his seatbelt and ducked down into a footwell.

All three vessels flew at top speed across the waves.

Alicia wouldn't just take it without retaliation. She held her right hand up and loosed off a few shots toward the boats. When the gunfire stalled for a short while, she glanced up.

Fuck it.

They were preparing to board. Even at speed, as the three boats raced. There were men lining up on the first vessel, ready to leap across. Alicia would let them. She laid down on her side, gun aimed, waiting for them to make the jump.

Seconds later, they did it. Hard-faced, swarthy men landed sure-footedly on Alicia's boat. They pinwheeled their arms for balance, and that was their undoing.

Alicia opened fire immediately, striking them in the chest. Her gun fired three times. Three red blooms appeared over the men's t-shirts and they flew back off the boat. Alicia rose swiftly, knowing the deaths of the three men would cause a distraction on the other boats.

She saw the dead men smash into the side of the racing boat. Their bodies collided with the craft and then they smashed down to the waves, disappearing beneath the blue seas forever. Alicia had just three shots left in her gun and she used them wisely, targeting the closest men with the biggest weapons on the nearest boat.

They went down too. Suddenly, the attacking boat seemed short of men. Alicia counted just four remaining besides the pilot.

And these four were approaching their gunwale at speed, readying to jump across. Alicia prepared to use her weapon as a club. Russo was suddenly beside her and then Crouch, joining from the rear. Another clipped burst of gunfire rang out, this time from the second boat, but the bullets all flew wildly by.

Their own boat hit a trough and then rose up. Alicia staggered. At that moment, the four attackers jumped. Because of the errant boat and the rise and fall of the sea, two men missed altogether, landing face first in the sea. One of them slapped up against the side of Alicia's boat, leaving a red smear in his wake. The other just disappeared.

Two men landed feet first on their boat. Both of them slipped immediately, falling back on their spines and letting out loud grunts. Their guns flew from their hands. Alicia didn't waste a moment, but scrambled after them, scooping one up for herself and throwing the other to Caitlyn.

The fallen men groaned, then tried to rise to their feet. Russo and Crouch shot them in the chest.

Now, the first chase boat swept away to be replaced by the second. The vessels were just feet apart, racing through the chop. Water fountained up between them, displaced by the vessels, and a great mist of spray hung over them.

Men shouted at them to surrender. Alicia just laughed. She checked her new gun. There were twelve bullets nestled in the mag, which was more than enough to take out the entire current chase boat.

She counted ten more men over there. For now, they were hiding as best they could, crouching beneath gunwales and sticking their heads out from other structures. They weren't firing, either. Alicia and her team conserved their bullet supply. The only people really doing anything were the two pilots.

Lanai was closing in.

The vast arc of a beach could be seen ahead now, the breakers rolling in towards the shore. Alicia couldn't see anyone on the beach, which was just as well, and had no idea where they were landing in relation to Kalani's position. She had to hope that Pierce did.

Alicia's mind flicked back to an earlier comment.

'Take out their engine,' she suddenly shouted. 'Like I said before, we can leave them dead in the water.'

Crouch and Russo immediately ran behind their own cockpit, aimed at the other boat, and opened fire. The enemy all ducked. Bullets rammed into the other boat, puncturing the glass-fibre and slamming into the heart of it. Crouch fired eight, Russo nine, until their guns were dry.

Caitlyn then immediately threw Russo the gun she'd received from Alicia. 'Nine in the mag,' she said.

But the extra bullets wouldn't be necessary. The other boat let out a great mechanical howl and then seemed to shudder. Immediately, it started slowing down. Alicia saw black smoke start billowing from underneath its engine hatch.

She cheered. The enemy then ran out on deck, sensing that something was wrong, and fired at Alicia's own boat. But by then, with Pierce keeping his hand on the throttle, they were pulling away. Alicia and the others ducked again to avoid any stray bullets.

The motorboat flew in towards the beach over the rolling waves.

In their wake, floundering, the 42K vessel slowed and then stopped. A fire broke out on board and the crew dashed for several extinguishers. Alicia imagined that someone would order the gang to swim in – those who could – but that would take them quite a while from their position.

Pierce kept the throttle open as their boat approached the shores of Lanai. The beach opened wide in a crescent shape. There was nowhere to hide the boat, but there was a thick treeline dead ahead.

Pierce did the best he could with their boat. He drove to the right, away from the floundering 42K vessel, and left it anchored at sea. It was the best he could do to keep it safe. They themselves would have to swim for a short while.

Alicia pocketed her gun and dived into the warm waters. It was balmy in there. Clear and fresh and more than tepid. She sliced her way through the incoming waves, sensing rather than seeing the others at her side. Soon, they had reached the shallows. Her feet touched the soft ground. Alicia rose and walked the last few yards to the sandy beach with the waves lapping at her ankles and water sluicing off her.

'Quite a sight,' Pierce said. He was already on shore.

'So I hear,' Alicia said. 'Don't get any ideas.'

'And why not?'

Alicia cocked her head. 'Can't you tell? I'm spoken for.'

'What the hell does that mean? That you have another guy in another port? I'm right here, right now, and I'm interested.'

Alicia regarded the PI. He wasn't shy around the women, that was for sure. Until now, though, she hadn't noticed his interest.

'Like I said, back off.'

'Yes, ma'am.'

'And for fuck's sake, don't start treating me with kid gloves. I'm a woman, not a piece of porcelain. Yeah, you've been rejected. Get over it. How about trying Caitlyn?'

'Not my type, unfortunately.'

'What about Russo?'

Pierce grinned and turned away. Alicia slapped him on the back. Together, they walked up the beach and stopped before the treeline.

'Do you have any idea where we are?' Crouch asked.

'Some,' Pierce said. 'We're on the opposite side of the island to Lanai City. More importantly, we're on the right side for Kalani. The old pineapple plantation where he's holed up is about eight klicks south of here.'

'And for us *non* military types?' Caitlyn asked.

'Oh, less than four miles. It shouldn't take long.'

'But it *will* give our persistent friends a chance to catch up,' Alicia said with a worried frown. 'And, at the last count, that's still about nine or ten armed men.'

'Then we go double time,' Pierce said. 'You ready?'

They were. They ran as if they were being hotly pursued, sweating in the heat, and soon they were dry, their clothes no longer sticking to them. Pierce led the way, seemingly a human compass, but then he had lived and worked on the island chain his entire life, often travelling between the islands.

Alicia let her thoughts turn to Kalani. Would they find him alive? Would he even let them help him?

And what did he really know of the great treasure they were hunting?

CHAPTER TWENTY FOUR

They raced for the pineapple plantation.

It was a long, hot, dusty trail, the ground choked with weeds and the fallen, broken branches of trees. Pierce led them as fast as he could, slowing often to skirt obstructions and once to find a break in a chain-link fence. They also crossed a wide road with no sign of vehicles travelling along it.

As they ran, Alicia checked her weapon.

She still had plenty of bullets, as did Russo, the only other of them now carrying a gun. They had no way of knowing how closely the 42K was following, but had to assume they would also be on foot. If they had access to a chopper, surely they'd have used that instead of powering to Lanai aboard boats. On the other hand, who knew what their bosses would do next?

Alicia hadn't seen Lynskey aboard either of the boats. Maybe the cop was too busy on Oahu, or just keeping a low profile. He knew they'd seen him, which was another reason the 42K were so interested in them. Lynskey wouldn't want his identity, his true purpose, known.

Speaking of that, Alicia sped up to Pierce's side.

'What do you plan to do about Lynskey?'

'I'll out the bastard as a rooked cop. But I can't do it whilst we search for Kalani. It has to be done the right way.'

'Good,' Alicia said. 'That's what I wanted to hear. We'll help as much as we can.'

Pierce nodded. He was walking at double-speed now, having taken a break from the running.

'What do you get out of all this?' he said after a while. 'Is it all about the final payoff?'

'Not even close,' Alicia said. 'I've never seen a penny from what Michael has found, and I don't want to. This is for friends, for my second family. I help them because they ask.'

'Nice attitude. Even Russo?'

Alicia laughed. 'He needs help more than most.'

Pierce shut up then and poured on more speed. Together, they ran across some arid landscape, pushing across endless fields where the pineapples had once been picked, running along the channels between the plants. It seemed to go on forever, but then Alicia saw a building materialise up ahead.

'Is that where he's staying?'

'That's where we *hope* he's staying. It's the biggest building on the plantation and it's quite vast. Keep your fingers crossed.'

'I have déjà-fucking-vu,' Alicia muttered.

'Over approaching Kalani? Yes, me too.'

'At least the 42K aren't on our asses.'

'Not yet.'

'Oh, that's looking on the bright side.'

'I like to stay realistic.'

They ran for the building, which was a long, low, squat building with a tiled roof. Clearly, it was a processing plant. Alicia knew the owners of the plantation would have a house somewhere too, but Pierce seemed not to be aware of that.

'Kalani!' Pierce started shouting out. 'Please come out! We need to talk!'

Alicia wondered again about the wisdom of shouting the kid's name, but then decided it was undoubtedly the best way to go. Even if he were here, he would see them and there were a thousand places to hide.

A great place to hide from the 42K.

Yes, this time she knew Kalani had done well for himself. Of course, he couldn't exactly survive on whatever pineapples still grew in the fields. He would still need supplies, but maybe he'd thought of that. Maybe he'd even brought some with him.

Pierce shouted his name again, and then twice more. The others joined in.

Alicia studied the extensive building. It had four different roofs, all pitched, and dozens of windows, all staring out over the plantation. At some time during the distant past, it had been a very busy, very productive processing building, probably housing dozens if not a hundred workers. Add to that the workers out on the field and you had an industrious plot of land right here.

Alicia watched the windows, hoping to see movement. She watched the doors. So far, Kalani wasn't playing ball.

If he was even here.

Alicia didn't like to think negatively. It didn't help anyone. She had to assume that Kalani was watching them right now and preparing to head out to meet them. *But why would he?* She thought. So far, all they'd done was to bring the 42K down on him.

She knew why he'd come out to meet them. Kalani wanted an end to all this, and they were the only people trying to help him. She believed he wanted to join them, to search for the treasure with them. He needed their aid. If Kalani chose any other way, he might end up dead.

Two minutes later, she saw a movement at one of the dilapidated doors. By now, she recognised the youth and the clothing he wore. Kalani was looking the worse for wear. They waited as he exited the building and walked towards them.

'I guess I shouldn't be surprised that you found me,' he said.

'We're plugged into the same network,' Pierce said.

'How come they always tell you, brah?'

'In my experience,' Pierce said. 'People only reveal secrets for three reasons. Friendship, money and coercion. People just like me.' Pierce gave him a wide grin.

'And if not, he greases their palms,' Alicia snorted. 'Or gives them a slap on the head.'

Pierce frowned at her. 'I know you're joking, but don't even think that. I've been connected since I could crawl. I recognised the advantages of face-to-face networking at a young age and have cultivated it ever since. I recall once putting the word out on a thief with the local nightclub bouncers, the cab drivers, the bellboys, and valets. Later that night, when I hooked up with a babe from Mililani Mauka, even *she* knew.'

'That's, um, sweet,' Alicia said. 'But hey, Kalani. Are you gonna run again, because we're running out of islands to hop over to, mate?'

Kalani gave her a weak smile. 'I am sorry,' he said. 'But I can't risk getting caught. They caught me once. It wasn't pleasant. If they catch me again, I fear the worst.'

'Your problem,' Pierce said. 'is that no matter who you call, *they* are plugged into the very same network. More or less,' he added.

'I understand that. But you have to understand how my life works.' Kalani shifted nervously from foot to foot. 'On the trust of friendship. I couldn't just move into the beach hut without getting permission. I couldn't camp on Akamu's old tribal lands without the right blessings and respect. Do you understand?'

Alicia got it, but still thought he was an idiot. If you were on the run, you didn't draw attention to yourself. If you were hiding, you didn't tell people *where*.

'And let's not forget *we* found you this time, too.' Crouch had half an eye on their rear and on the landscape all around. 'We encountered the 42K on the way here.'

Kalani's eyes bulged, and he turned round and round, going into flight mode. Alicia could tell that he wanted to bolt.

'Listen,' she said. 'We took care of at least half of them. And we left the rest adrift in the ocean. All they could do was swim here, and that'd take time.'

'But they're coming,' Kalani said.

'Look,' Crouch stepped forward. 'We have an entirely different problem to think about. The way out of all this is to produce Kamehameha. Are you ready to go on a treasure hunt?'

Kalani stopped turning. 'I want to do that,' he said. '*I want to*. But it's too dangerous.'

'Not if you stick with us,' Crouch stepped forward. 'This is what we do. We've found Aztec gold, pirate gold, galleon's gold, you name it, against overwhelming odds. If you come with us, we can keep you safe.'

Kalani didn't look convinced. First, he glanced at Pierce, and then at the building behind him. 'I've survived this long,' he said a little sullenly.

'By the skin of your knack... teeth,' Alicia bit her tongue halfway through the comment.

'You might have led them straight to me,' Kalani wouldn't be mollified.

Alicia was getting impatient with the kid. Here, they were busting their nuts to save his ass and all he could do was blame them and moan about it. This King Kamehameha, she decided, better be worth all the bloody effort.

'Hey,' Russo had been silent until now, but suddenly spoke up.

Alicia ignored the big oaf. 'So Kalani, if you've finished your island tour, maybe you can—'

'Hey!' Russo whispered.

Alicia whirled on him. 'Jesus Christ, Russo, if you need the toilet, just go.'

Russo was peering through the trees at their backs. His face was grim. 'I saw something.'

And then they heard something.

Alicia turned her face towards the skies. 'Oh, shit.'

CHAPTER TWENTY FIVE

The heavy thud of rotor blades thumped at the air.

Alicia looked above the treeline, saw nothing yet, but knew their nemesis on this mission was closing in. She took out her gun, habitually checking the mag even though she knew exactly what was in there. Russo did the same.

'Take cover,' Crouch said.

Kalani, now that he had to, could barely move. 'Are they here?' he asked.

'Yeah, and more than we expected,' Alicia was still searching for the approaching chopper. 'Now, move.'

They ran for the extensive building, aiming for the same door Kalani had stepped out of. Before they could reach it, the chopper swept over the treeline and hovered over the clearing in front of the building. Alicia looked up. Men were hanging out of it on both sides, all carrying weapons.

'And they have new firepower,' she said.

She saw AK 47's, H&K's, and even an RPG bristling from the sides of the chopper. She looked ahead, knowing they'd never reach the shelter in time. Above, the men took aim.

And fired. Bullets spattered into the ground, raising puffs of smoke where they hit, which was to left and right of the running men and women. Caitlyn staggered, but Crouch caught her. Kalani was first to the door.

Alicia brought up the rear. She hadn't opened fire yet, and neither had Russo. Both of them saw the prudence of conserving ammo. The chopper roared above them, getting lower and lower.

More bullets pounded the ground. Alicia was directly under descending aircraft, safe, but Russo was close to getting hit. It was Michael who slowed, reached down, grabbed a rock and threw it up at the helicopter's windscreen.

The rock clanged off, leaving a scratch in the glass. The chopper wavered, its men forced to hang on and stop firing. Alicia and the rest of her team dashed into the building, temporarily under cover.

'How many?' Russo called out.

'I counted at least eight,' Alicia replied. 'With more in the fields. And a lot of firepower.'

'They got reinforcements from Oahu,' Pierce said. 'It makes sense.'

Kalani hopped from one foot to the other. 'We can't stay here,' he said.

Alicia looked at him. 'The kid's right. Where does this building lead to?'

They all turned to Kalani.

'Well, all the others,' he said. 'There's at least five buildings here, all connected by walkways or bridges or passages. It's a warren.'

'You've explored it?' Crouch asked. When Kalani nodded, he said, 'Well, that puts us one step ahead of our enemy.'

The sound of the chopper putting down outside was loud, the roar of a feral beast. Some men aboard were firing into the building's block walls just for the hell of it, or targeting and smashing the windows. Alicia expected nothing less of brain-dead thugs. But that didn't make them any less dangerous.

'We have to move,' she said.

Through one window, they could see to the far side of the plantation. They saw more men now threading through the treeline, at least six. 'I reckon the count's at fourteen now,' she said. 'Maybe more.'

'Those will be the ones we left in the water,' Crouch said.

Kalani looked too panicked to lead them. He didn't know which way to turn, to look, to run. That kind of attitude, Alicia knew, could get you dead real quick.

'Which way?' Pierce pressed him.

They had no time left. Men were running at the open door. Through the window, Alicia saw one figure bend down on one knee and heft the grenade launcher across his right shoulder.

'RPG!' she yelled and hit the floor.

There was a shocked, seemingly endless second and then the rocket struck the front of the building, just above the window. The frame just withered away under the force. Block and mortar and bricks exploded into the building from the point of impact. Part of the front of the building sagged.

'The roof's coming down!' Kalani screamed.

Alicia jumped up. She could see outside far easier now and saw the man with the grenade launcher prepping another rocket.

'Shit,' she scrambled backward and hit the floor again. Seconds later, there was another impact. This one made the entire building shudder. Dust and plaster and other debris flew in clouds towards the floor. More mortar and shrapnel rushed inside the building. The hole above the window expanded rapidly.

Alicia coughed, surrounded by plumes of dust. She lifted her head. There was a great swirling cloud between her and the various doors and windows that lined the front of the building.

And then she saw approaching shadows through the gloom.

There was nothing else for it. Although she only had eight bullets, Alicia was forced to open fire. She saved the shots for certain kills; waited until the men crowded the entrance and then fired at their centre of mass. She took two of them down immediately.

Which sent the others scrambling back. For now.

Alicia jumped up, waving at the clouds that drifted around her. Unless they moved fast, this was going to get deadly serious. At the moment, between her and Russo, they had enough bullets to take care of their assailants, but she knew that wouldn't last.

Crouch yelled at Kalani, asking him the right way to go. Kalani pointed. They jumped up and ran through the building, heading for a back door. They covered the ground swiftly, aware that their enemy might come through the front doors at any moment.

And then they did.

Guns out, wearing body armour, they filed through the doors as one. They were taking no chances. Alicia realised her bullets, aimed at the chests of the two men, might not have taken them out. Suddenly, this whole thing had risen a notch. She aimed her next bullet at a man's head.

And missed.

The bullet flew inches past his skull, but it made him flinch and hit the floor, along with most of his colleagues.

Crouch and Kalani reached the back of the enormous building. Kalani pointed at a half-open door. Crouch pushed through at a run. Alicia and the others sprinted after them.

And that was when the shooting began in earnest. Bullets chased them as they approached the door and then squeezed through.

Alicia slammed it closed behind her, thankful it was strong and sturdy. Several bullets thwacked into the steel door and the block work from the other side of the wall. She turned, saw Kalani and Crouch rushing through a wide room crammed full of old furniture, and followed.

Then, through the thick walls, Alicia heard another noise. It was the roar of the chopper again, lifting off. She didn't like it, unsure what her enemy had in mind, but knowing it wouldn't be good.

The roar continued, louder now. Alicia threaded her way through an accumulation of desks and chairs and tables and old couches. It seemed they had packed the entire complex's furniture into one room. At her back, she heard the door grinding open.

'Faster,' she said.

Ahead, Kalani tripped and fell. Alicia whirled and put two bullets at head-height into the men coming through the door. Two figures screamed and flew backward, seriously hit. Good shots, but she was now down to just three bullets.

Russo signalled that he'd change places with her.

Alicia ran ahead, closing in on the fallen Kalani.

'He's okay,' Crouch said.

'Then get moving.'

They hauled the Hawaiian to his feet and approached another door at the far end of the room. This one was currently closed, matted with cobwebs and covered in dust. Just then, the sound of the helicopter got louder, making them all look up to the roof.

'What is it doing?' Caitlyn asked.

They didn't have to wait long to find out.

Because, suddenly, the ceiling exploded.

CHAPTER TWENTY SIX

Alicia couldn't believe her eyes.

They must have a second RPG, and had fired it straight down into the roof above. The rocket impacted and detonated, shattering through the tiles and felt and plasterboard. Wreckage collapsed into the room like a deadly waterfall, bringing with it shards of tiles and lengths of timber. There was nowhere to hide. Luckily, the main force of the implosion was away to their right, closer to the side of the building. There, it was devastation, everything just collapsing. The entire roof sagged above them, held up now by the skills of the people who'd built it rather than anything engineered.

Kalani dragged the far door open.

The others, ducking and swaying, ran for it. They pushed through. A quick glance back showed that their pursuers hadn't been deterred. They were still coming, pushing through and skirting whatever rubble had fallen into the room.

The next room, the third part of the five-roofed building, was a kitchen area. A stained old sink and draining board stood off to the right, a chair and tables to the left; lots of cabinets lined the walls. Alicia ran to a chair, picked it up and wedged it under the door handle.

'Every second counts,' she said.

Kalani ran but then slowed, noting there were three doors to choose from. Alicia saw him dithering. She bit her lip. This wasn't good. She raced through her companions until she stood at his side.

'Which fucking way,' she growled.

Kalani looked blank, but then pointed at the middle door. 'That way.'

Alicia pushed him towards it. Just then, several things happened at once. Men burst in from the previous room after smashing into the door until her makeshift obstacle scraped out of the way. These men were firing as they came, their bullets flying haphazardly in all directions. At the same time, the helicopter above yet again made its presence known.

There was another resounding explosion.

And the roof fell in once more. This time, it was even more devastating. Alicia flew forward and pushed her and Kalani through the door. Bullets skimmed past them. Above, the ceiling collapsed in a downward flurry of debris, shattering to the floor. It smashed among her team, something striking Crouch across the shoulders, a piece of timber glancing off Russo's skull, sending him to his knees, a cloud of dust completely enveloping Caitlyn.

Alicia was clear on the other side of the door.

She turned back, tugging at the door handle, but, since the frame was now skewed with the impact from above, she couldn't open it.

Above, she heard the chopper manoeuvring its way into place.

'How many times are the bastards gonna bomb the damn roof?' Alicia yelled. 'I thought they wanted you alive.'

'Something's changed,' Kalani said.

Alicia was torn. On the one side, she couldn't get the door open to go to the aid of her colleagues. On the other, she knew that there were two more doors they could hopefully use, which would put them in another room. And on a third side, she could hear the helicopter roaring above them.

'Move,' she decided.

They ran quickly, just in time, because their pursuers suddenly rattled the door behind them. *Good luck with that,* Alicia thought, but then heard the clunk of a grenade against the metal and ran harder, ducking her head.

'*Duck!*' she yelled.

The grenade detonated, blasting a hole through the door. Alicia staggered forward, stunned by the sound but still propelled towards the next door. Kalani was a step in front of her.

They raced into another room, this one thankfully empty. At the far end, Alicia spied a set of stairs.

'There,' Kalani said.

'We go up?'

'Yes, there's a walkway that will take us to the next building and then it's a maze.'

'Where we can hide?'

'That's right.'

'Always assuming they don't just bury us beneath the rubble,' she said with a lot of sarcasm.

She was on edge, fuming, annoyed at being separated from her colleagues. She was anxious about their safety, wondering how they were doing. But, for now, she had to focus. They raced through the room, reached the bottom of the stairs by the time the door behind them opened. Alicia ran up a few steps, then turned and fired again, which put her dwindling supply of bullets down to two.

Again, she scored a success. One man flew back into the doorframe, blood spearing from the back of his head and coating his companions. To a man, they all threw themselves to the ground.

More time gained. Alicia climbed the stairs at double speed, chasing Kalani. The young thief leapt onto the top step and slammed into a pair of double glass doors. Luckily for him, they were unlocked and flew open, smashing back into a double metal railing.

Alicia joined him. They were one floor up, facing a long metal walkway that ran between two buildings. The walkway was wide open and would leave them exposed for a short period.

No other way.

They couldn't go back. Their enemies were already approaching the stairs below.

Alicia motioned Kalani onto the walkway. There were handrails running along both sides. Kalani grabbed one and started walking, his boots clanking on the metal surface. The whole thing swayed as he walked, and Alicia bit her lip. She'd never been very good at heights.

Kalani walked carefully forward. Alicia counted to five and then followed. They needed to move swiftly, but the state of the walkway screamed caution. Alicia stepped carefully at Kalani's back, her boots ringing on the screeching metal.

'Have you already been across this?' she asked.

'Once. Thought it was super dangerous.'

Alicia shook her head. 'Cheers, man.'

They took it a step at a time, taking no chances. They were just over halfway across when the double doors crashed open again and men came flooding out of the staircase area. Alicia looked back, counted five of them. Immediately, they raised their weapons.

'Stop there!'

Alicia gave them the finger and kept walking.

'Stop now!'

Another step, and then another. They were three quarters of the way across by now.

One man fired, his aim deliberately high. Alicia still felt the scorch of the bullet as it blasted past her skull. Too close for comfort. At that moment, she saw the helicopter drift into sight to her right, rising to look at the two people crossing the walkway. It came in nose first, its rotors blasting the air apart.

Alicia kept moving. They were beset on all sides now.

Behind them, the men had had enough. Alicia sensed it. She span and fired a shot, making them scatter. She urged Kalani on. There was nowhere to go. The men crowded the walkway now, aiming their guns at her.

Alicia fired her last bullet, striking a man in the neck.

They all raised their weapons and targeted her.

And incredibly, in that moment, something happened that not even Alicia could have predicted. It was crazy, beyond madness. The idling helicopter swung slightly to its right; a man leaned out of the cabin. In his hand, he held the dreaded RPG.

He took aim at the walkway and fired.

Alicia saw it coming too late. She yelled a warning, but then the rocket struck behind her, about a quarter of the way down the metal causeway, and exploded, spitting fire. Some of the 42K men were caught by the flames and collapsed; others scrambled away, their flesh burnt. Where the rocket hit, the walkway collapsed.

It fell away from Alicia.

But she wasn't done. Using her last few inches of momentum, even as the metal fell away beneath her, she grabbed hold of Kalani and swung with it, travelling in a wide arc. She kept a tight hold on Kalani. Her momentum swung her toward the next building, falling sharply but propelled forward, and she smashed through one of the windows at high speed. She felt the glass shatter, saw the concrete floor coming, tucked and rolled, still holding onto the Hawaiian. He screamed and squirmed and rolled with her, the two coming to a stop in an ungainly heap.

'You're crazy!' he yelled into her ear.

'So I've been told. Hold on to your balls, Kalani. This isn't over yet.'

The young Hawaiian reached between his legs. 'Why? What the hell do you plan to do next?'

CHAPTER TWENTY SEVEN

Alicia grunted and slapped his hands away.

'It was metaphorical,' she said. 'A phrase us indestructible action heroes use when we've just escaped certain death.'

Kalani struggled to his feet. 'Oh, I thought you were serious.'

'Listen,' she looked left and right. 'I've bought us a few minutes, but we have to get back to the crew. This separation isn't good.'

'They had two rooms to choose from,' Kalani remembered. 'A lounge and a storage room. Both lead deeper into the house. But they both exit through a large kitchen in the rear, almost a prep room. Come with me.'

Kalani led her through a dingy room and he turned left, angling back to the main house. Alicia was worried they'd bump into more of the 42K goons, but right now her bruises and aches and scrapes were her top priority. She checked herself for injuries as she loped after Kalani.

After a while, she determined all was okay. She still held on to the gun, though it was empty, in case she needed a club or a missile. It was one of those things that was better to have than not. This time, she followed Kalani unerringly, trusting that he knew his way.

'Hopefully,' he said. 'They'll be right along here.'

They traversed a long hallway. At the far end, there was a narrow picture window hung with fraying drapes. It was as they raced along this passage that the man stepped out of a room.

Not one of their companions.

Alicia sped up, trying to get ahead of Kalani. The man turned to them. He was holding a knife. Kalani slowed, head going backward.

'Fall,' Alicia suddenly shouted. 'Drop, *now.*'

Luckily, Kalani got it. He flung himself to the ground and slid towards the guy. Alicia kept up the pace and leapt over his sliding figure, knees forward, striking her enemy in the torso. He brought a hand up to defend himself, but Alicia's momentum drove him back towards the picture window. He crashed into it, breaking it. Shards showered the floor.

Alicia landed heavily on her knees. Pain shot through her body. Despite hitting the window hard, the man swung at her with his knife, which she deftly ducked. The knife struck the side wall, carving out a chunk of plaster.

Alicia came up with a knee strike, connecting hard with the guy's midriff. She followed that up with devastating punches to the throat and face and a massive clout across the temple with her gun. The man's legs went instantly weak, and he slipped to the floor.

Kalani was still behind her. A miracle. She grabbed him by the shirt.

'Which way?'

He pointed. She crept carefully through another door into a large, empty room, crossed that and entered yet another. The dank smell of mould permeated the entire area. Cobwebs hung low in every corner. Dust coated the floor. At the moment, she could hear nothing but their own harsh, low breathing.

Alicia reached the next door. Through it, she could hear noise. Carefully, she peered through the gap. 'Thank fuck,' she said. 'Michael.'

The others were clustered inside a tiny utility room, and were clearly discussing where to go next. Russo raised his gun when he heard a noise, but soon lowered it when he saw Alicia.

'Where the hell did you go?' he snapped.

'Aw, did you miss me, mate? Nobody to look after you?'

Crouch had turned when she spoke his name. Now he just looked relieved. 'Are you both okay?'

Alicia nodded, entering the room. 'As well as can be expected after what we've just been through.'

Kalani then stepped forward. 'There's a way out of this house,' he said. 'Through there,' he pointed at a back door. 'And then between utility buildings. It's dark and twisty, but I know the way. It might just be intricate enough to throw our friends off the trail.'

Crouch grinned. 'Then lead the bloody way, mate.'

Their accents might have thrown Kalani, but he knew an invitation when he heard one. He squeezed through the utility, carefully opened the back door and disappeared outside. Russo followed him closely, then Crouch, with Alicia now bringing up the rear. Listening hard, she heard nothing except their own movements, but it was a vast house. The 42K could be anywhere.

Outside, the early afternoon sunlight was hot and bright. Dust motes drifted through the air. Kalani led them over an open patch of dry ground into a dark passageway formed by the backs of two other buildings. The passageway was humid and took a few moments to get used to.

They stalked down the passageway to where both buildings ended and more began. They were at a kind of junction, a junction of high brick walls. Kalani preceded them down the left branch to another and then cut right, leading them – as far as Alicia could tell – northward. Soon, she felt lost, surrounded by the buildings, not knowing which way was which, guided by Kalani and the sun.

A while later, they emerged from the other side of the huddle of buildings. They faced a wide pineapple field bordered by a bushy hedge at the far end. Kalani pointed at it.

'The road is just beyond that hedge,' he said.

Crouch blinked at him. 'Where's the nearest town?' he asked.

'No towns. Just settlements. Farms. My friend has a place just over that rise, about three miles away.'

Alicia put a hand on his shoulder. 'Is that the same friend you told you were lying low at the plantation?'

Kalani's face fell. 'You think...'

'Money's a great motivator,' Alicia said. 'Who else could it have been?'

Kalani faltered a little. 'Oh crap, then I've led you on a road to nowhere. The only town is Lanai City, on the opposite side of the island.'

Alicia saw the others look downcast. She listened hard, but there were no sounds of pursuit, no sounds at all, in fact. It was so silent; the stillness resonated in their ears.

It was Crouch who turned to the buildings. 'What's in them?' he asked. 'Any cars? Vehicles of any kind?'

Kalani nodded. 'Of course. This was a busy, working plantation. They have tons of vehicles.'

'I understand you don't know this,' Crouch said. 'But military operatives like Alicia, Russo and I are trained in methods of resurrecting any vehicle that might have been abandoned or just left at the side of the road. It's a skill that comes in handy when you're behind enemy lines, in the middle of nowhere, and need a ride to freedom. They taught us to mend just about anything.'

Kalani nodded. 'Let me show you.'

Soon they were being shown a couple of buildings like barns, where some of the old plantation vehicles had been stored. Alicia saw dusty old trucks, cars and a couple of large lorries. Crouch made a beeline for the nearest, smallest truck that would take all of them, an old Chevy.

'Take the watch,' Crouch told Alicia. 'Russo and I will handle this.'

Alicia nodded, slipped back outside. The view to the front was just one extensive field and then the high hedge. To either side, the doors and walls of buildings spread in both directions. She stayed close to the wall, relying on her sense of hearing.

Should she be upbeat?

They had secured Kalani, a major plus. But now the 42K were everywhere and had brought in extra firepower, proving they were deadly serious. She wondered if more were on their way.

All this to grab Kalani and the secret to Kamehameha.

Alicia stayed in the large shadow afforded by the building. She heard nothing. After about twenty minutes, Crouch called her back inside the barn.

'We think we're ready,' he said, cleaning his hands on an old rag. 'We've cleaned and run fuel through everything we can. Open the doors wide. This old bus is gonna rattle and shake when we start her up.'

Which would bring the 42K running. Alicia undid the latches and pulled up the ground locks and then put her shoulder to one of the doors. It was stiff, time having fixed it into place. At first, it wouldn't budge but, as Alicia put more and more pressure behind it, the door ground open. She pushed the left side wide open and then the right and then made her way over to the waiting vehicle.

'How do we get through the hedge?' she asked.

'We go fast,' Crouch replied.

'Okay then. Sounds like you have everything worked out.'

Crouch took a deep breath, twisted a few wires together and then made a face. 'Give me a minute,' he said, bending down to look under the wheel.

They waited. Crouch checked his work. Inside, the barn was intensely hot. Alicia could hear the sounds of birds nesting. That was okay. She didn't mind birds. It was creepy-crawlies that bothered her.

Crouch straightened. He said, 'Let's try this again,' and twisted some more wires. This time, the truck roared into life, belching black smoke and juddering like a man high on caffeine. Alicia tried to stay still as the whole cabin shook.

Crouch engaged first gear with a grinding crack.

'Hang on,' he said.

They started moving forward. The only thing they couldn't be too sure about was the state of the tyres, though none were flat. The truck bounced and juddered through the barn and passed between the main doors.

Into the sunlight. Alicia grabbed the dash and held on. Crouch picked up speed. They juddered among the pineapple rows, heading straight for a thinner point of the hedge and the road beyond. Crouch kept his foot to the floor. The truck bounced even harder as it got faster, throwing its occupants around. The rutted field didn't help. Alicia saw a cloud of dust rising from their rear.

So if the noise didn't attract the 42K, the mushroom cloud certainly would.

But Crouch kept them going, pumping the clutch and the accelerator. If they stalled now, they'd be in deadly trouble. Alicia watched the side mirrors but saw no sign of the 42K.

The hedge came up fast. As promised, Crouch hit it at speed, tearing apart intertwined branches and busting through. The truck shuddered hard as it smashed the hedge apart and travelled up a slight slope before emerging onto the narrow road.

Crouch swung the wheel to the left as directed by Kalani.

Caitlyn cheered.

They were free of the plantation, Alicia knew. But were they free of the 42K?

CHAPTER TWENTY EIGHT

The old truck rattled down the narrow road, hedges to both sides. Alicia could feel the softness of the tyres, hear the clunk of the engine, sense the reluctance of the vehicle, and wondered if it would get them even another mile. But Crouch kept on coaxing it, and Russo patted its dash, smiling as he did so.

'That's the happiest I've ever seen you,' Alicia said to him. 'You have a thing for old junk, Rob?'

'If I did, I'd be dating you, Alicia.'

She laughed. She let him have that one, not just because it made her laugh, but because Russo's antics actually seemed to work. The truck soldiered on.

Ten minutes later, Kalani's voice sounded from the back seat. 'Oh, no. That can't be good.'

Alicia checked the side mirror and felt her heart sink. It was the one thing they'd all feared. The 42K hadn't bothered finding a vehicle. They'd all piled back into the chopper instead. Now, it was racing along the road after them, maybe thirty feet high, following the line of the hedge and the road. Its sides were festooned with bodies, people hanging out the open doors and crowded inside. The chopper looked top heavy, barely able to rise above the thirty feet, and the men hung on tightly to their precarious handholds.

'Put your foot down,' Alicia said automatically.

'No way is this old crate gonna outrun them,' Crouch said. 'Get ready for a fight.'

Alicia swore. 'No weapons,' she said. 'Unless I take my boots off and throw them.'

'I have six bullets left,' Russo told her.

'A tactical decision,' Alicia said. 'Do we shoot them *before* they harry us, or *as* they harry us?'

'Whatever happens, I'm not slowing down,' Crouch shouted above the clatter of the engine.

The chopper swooped in their wake, getting closer and closer. Alicia was next to the window, so Russo handed her the gun. She turned in her seat, cranked the window down and leaned out.

Aimed the handgun.

The pilot saw her and reacted quickly. She didn't shoot. The chopper veered away, across the adjacent field and then looped back around. Now it hovered a few hundred yards in their wake. Alicia assumed the pilot would get fresh orders.

Crouch approached a junction in the road. Kalani told him to take the right fork. They didn't slow. The road was incredibly quiet, though the island was small and sparsely populated. Crouch rounded the bend at speed. Alicia winced as all the nuts and bolts holding the car together squealed in protest.

The helicopter tracked them, inching closer. Alicia still had her head out of the window and the gun in her hand. She raised it again. This time, the chopper didn't shy away; it kept coming. This time – the men hanging out of it pointed weapons of their own.

Alicia fired first, just one shot. She'd been aiming at the pilot, but the sway of the aircraft and the juddering of the truck threw her aim off. The bullet instead struck one of the men leaning out of the chopper and sent him tumbling away to the ground, falling like a stone. The helicopter, on losing a man, didn't miss a beat.

It kept coming.

And now more men were leaning out, their weapons aimed. They didn't hesitate to open fire. Alicia ducked back inside as bullets slammed into the road and hedges all around them, as shots peppered the rear of the truck with a loud popping sound.

'Shit, this isn't working,' Crouch yelled.

He slammed the brakes on, probably hoping they still worked. They caught hard, bringing the truck to a sudden halt. The chopper clattered overheard, flying into the distance before banking. Crouch put his foot down and started the truck moving forward again.

'What exactly did that accomplish?' Alicia asked.

'Absolutely fucking nothing.' Crouch said. 'It was a gut reaction to get them off our asses.'

'Now they're in front of us,' Alicia said.

'I'm aware of that.'

There was nothing Crouch could do except keep going. The helicopter had turned and was now racing at them with its nose down, flying just above the hedges. There were men hanging out on both sides, weapons raised.

'Shit!' Alicia yelled.

The two vehicles converged. Bullets spattered the truck, striking the bonnet and the roof. The windscreen smashed, glass shattering inward. Alicia could only duck down into the footwell as the others threw themselves across the back seats.

Then the helicopter was past. Alicia was quick to react, leaning out the window again and firing another shot that took another man out of the action. He also plummeted to the ground. But nothing would now deter the chopper. It started after them again, its rotors buffeting the air hard. It was a big black bird of prey, a predator at their heels. It closed the gap rapidly and, again; the men opened fire.

This time, bullets rattled the truck from front to back. Kalani yelled out that they were just twenty minutes from the town if they could hang on.

But it wasn't to be.

Almost inevitably, a bullet found its way into the engine. Whatever it did in there, it was lethal and it was permanent. A black plume of smoke billowed up from under the bonnet, obscuring their vision. The truck started slowing down.

Crouch slammed the wheel hard. 'Nowhere to go,' he said.

As the truck slowed, Alicia put her hand on the door. The only way out of here was speed and aggression. She was good with both. The chopper was hovering at their rear now, just waiting for them to come to a dead stop.

Which soon happened. The truck died bit by bit, failing at the side of the road. Alicia and the others rammed open the doors and rushed out. Behind them, keeping its distance, the chopper settled in the middle of the road.

'Run!' Crouch and Pierce cried at the same time.

They didn't run together. They split up to keep the enemy guessing. Alicia and Caitlyn ran to the left, leapt down a small slope and then got on their knees to climb through the hedge. Behind them, they could hear men shouting, most of them yelling Kalani's name.

The young thief was caught like a deer in the headlights.

It was only now that Alicia saw him running away from the truck at an angle. This was the reason the men from the helicopter weren't shooting at anything. New orders. All their attention was on Kalani. Most of them were already in pursuit. Alicia saw Pierce standing with his arms out, looking as if Kalani had torn away from him and gone his own way.

Alicia counted fifteen 42K, all armed. She had four bullets left. She didn't stand a chance. The others had no weapons between them. They couldn't save Kalani.

She saw the 42K giving chase. Two men fired just above Kalani's head, slowing him down. Now they caught up faster, all fifteen of them racing through the fields. The men were grim faced and sweating profusely, but they were determined. They had their orders. They chased Kalani down and kicked him to the floor, where two of them delivered a few more kicks for good measure. Alicia saw Kalani squirming.

'What can we do?' Caitlyn fretted.

Alicia hated to say it. 'Nothing. If we were armed like them, I'd give it a go. But, at the moment, we're just lucky they've left us alone to go after Kalani.'

'Not lucky for him,' Caitlyn said miserably.

Alicia agreed. 'I don't see what else we can do.'

They watched as Kalani was dragged to his feet and then shoved in the back. Men crowded around him. One of them punched him in the ribs, much to the consternation of another, who waved him away. Clearly, they wanted Kalani mobile, able to walk. Alicia raised her gun, torn between two nasty options.

Let it happen, or die trying to save him.

And possibly see Caitlyn, Crouch, Pierce and Russo die too. At the moment, they were all crouching amid the pineapple rows; the leaves giving them some cover, basically meaning that they were out of sight, out of mind. Alicia watched the helicopter's pilot for a few seconds, saw him focused on the approaching group of men.

'We can't save Kalani,' she reiterated, torn inside.

'But they'll kill him.'

'We're not out of options yet. We still have Pierce.'

Caitlyn swore as they watched Kalani led to the chopper, hauled on board and then secured between men. Soon, the craft was roaring, its rotors shredding air, and then it started moving, taking Kalani with it.

A minute later it was gone, headed west.

Alicia and the others came out of their hiding places.

'Got any bright ideas?' Crouch asked.

CHAPTER TWENTY NINE

Kalani tried to remain absolutely still. He'd been sandwiched between two men, riding in the back of the chopper, with other enemies all around him. Their faces were sweaty and dirty and forbidding, some slicked with blood. None of them looked the slightest bit happy. Kalani's chest hurt, his ribs ached where he'd been punched and kicked, but he stayed as still as he could.

Terrible thoughts ran through his head.

After all this, after everything he'd done, the 42K had still caught him. Was it his fault? Was it Pierce's? Did it really matter?

Kalani knew there was no way he could have outrun the criminals indefinitely. He didn't have enough places to go, and they were all plugged into the same networks. Well, they were all around him now, much too close for comfort. He wondered what they intended to do with him.

Oddly, they were headed away from Oahu, so he wasn't being taken back to the 42K's principal base. Maybe the cops who ran the gang had another secret hideout. Maybe Kalani was being taken there.

He shivered. Things couldn't be much worse. He knew beyond any doubt that the moment he led them to Kamehameha's remains, his life was forfeit.

So what next?

Find another way to escape. Yes, that would be best, but not travelling at fifty feet in the air.

What would MacGyver do?

Kalani recalled watching several TV programmes where the protagonist was spirited away in a helicopter. Was there a clue there for him? Could he remember what happened and work something out? Kalani felt sorry that he was in this situation. He knew it was mostly of his own devising. There was a step in the Hawaiian cycle of repentance that he knew well. He'd thought about it often. Ho'oponopono assumed you were responsible for everything in your own mind, whether or not it was crazy and undisciplined. Once you accepted that thought, it was easier to become sorry.

Kalani was sorry for an awful lot right now. And he accepted the fault was all his.

He held tight as the chopper ploughed on through the mid-afternoon. The sun blazed in through the windows and the open doors. The men all around him didn't say much, just held on and stared ahead. The chopper swooped down as it left land, skimming across the tops of the waves and heading out into the ocean. It was a beautiful mirror blue down there, and Kalani could see the black helicopter reflected in it. He looked ahead, remained quiet, and finally saw the land mass that was coming up.

Maui. The second largest of the Hawaiian islands.

Kalani knew Maui was a major hub and a tourist hotspot. It had several towns, some of them large, and its own local criminal element. It was perfectly possible that Lynskey and his corrupt cop friends could have an operation ongoing there.

The chopper glided across the tops of the waves, so close Kalani could see the swells and taste the saltwater in the air. It didn't slow as it reached Maui, but flew in over the land mass at speed and banked to the east across a stand of palm trees and low houses. Kalani heard the pilot talking on the radio.

'We're coming in hot right now,' he said.

'You have Kalani?' clearly they were not trying to stay under the radar.

'Yeah, keep it low key. We don't want anyone to recover this information except the 42K.'

'Got it.'

Kalani's hands balled up into fists. Whatever was going to happen to him wasn't far away. The 42K had already proven what an evil entity they were. Now, Kalani was in their grasp, at their mercy.

The chopper touched down, its skids bouncing three times off a hard-packed yard. It looked like they'd landed on a small farmstead. There was a large house and fields all around, other outbuildings too. There were separate buildings dotted around the wider area, but none were close enough to hear a man scream.

Kalani shook the thought out of his head. He had a major decision to make. If he told the 42K what they wanted to know, there would be less pain, and he'd probably live longer, giving him more chance to make his escape. If he didn't tell them what they wanted to know, he'd be beaten, tortured, and more.

The helicopter settled. The men started exiting. One of them took hold of Kalani by the right arm and started dragging him out. Kalani's boots left the chopper and hit the hard dirt, then went stumbling towards the house. There were more of them here – lots of youths in their t-shirts and jackets and jeans and shorts, all carrying their guns and knives, all lounging and staring and uncaring of his tenuous position.

Kalani stumbled along the path and then went through the front door. The inside of the house was dark and dingy, uninviting. Oak panelling covered the walls. They led Kalani down a long narrow hallway to the back, where they pushed him into a white painted room in which were set two plastic chairs and a table.

It looked like a police interview room.

Kalani turned to his captor, a black-haired pockmarked man with one lazy eye and an expression like a Great White hunting its prey.

'What happens next?' he asked. 'What do you want with me?'

The man shrugged. 'Don't know, don't care,' he said in the native tongue. 'You sit and wait.'

Kalani watched the man go, heard him lock the door. He looked around. There were no windows, no other doors, no way out unless he tunnelled through the floor. If only he had a penknife, he would do exactly that. Kalani didn't want to sit; he'd been sitting aboard the chopper for the best part of forty minutes. He wanted to walk, so he paced and paced, from one side of the room to the other, trying to get some sort of story right in his head.

It surprised him when, fifteen minutes later, the door opened. That was quick.

But he was in for another surprise. They had brought him a sandwich and a bottle of water. The man with the lazy eye placed the items on the table and then withdrew. Kalani eyed them. Did that mean he was going to be waiting here for a while?

He ate and drank. Why not? It would keep his strength up and it helped take his mind off the bare-faced fear he was experiencing. Here he was, deep in the enemy camp, at their mercy, and what could he do? What would *Magnum* do?

Somehow, all his TV heroes would contrive a way to escape.

Kalani had already decided that was what he was going to do, but he couldn't do it here, stuck in this room.

Hours later, they returned. Kalani had no way of knowing what time it was, how long had passed between visits. This time Lazy Eye brought with him two men. One of them, dressed weirdly in a white suit, stood near the door, his back to the far wall, and watched proceedings. The other was a far different prospect.

As soon as he set eyes on him, Kalani knew that this man was his torturer.

He nicknamed him the Rake because of his scrawniness. Yes, he was a spindly creature, his thinness enhanced because of his height. He had long lank locks that fell to his shoulders, unkempt facial hair, and he sweated a lot. He was sweating as he approached Kalani, and his lips were dry to the point of cracking and bleeding. When he spoke, spit flew from his lips.

'Tell us what we want to know.' He whispered breathily.

Kalani fought to hide his fear. 'What is that?'

'You escaped before,' the man hissed. 'It won't happen again. Go on. Try.' He backed away, held out his arms. He was clearly enjoying himself.

Kalani knew this was all part of the torture. Something devised to instil despair. He looked from the Rake to Lazy Eye to White Suit and knew he could never get past them all. And of course, if he did, there were a hundred others, all armed.

'You choose how this goes,' the Rake said. 'I don't mind either way.'

'Tell me exactly what you want,' Kalani said through dry lips.

The Rake balled up a fist and struck Kalani across the face. He stepped in and punched Kalani on the chin. Two more hard fists came in then, each one directed at Kalani's chest. He could barely breathe, but he fought not to slide out of his chair. He wouldn't give the Rake that kind of satisfaction.

'You hold the secret to a great treasure,' the Rake stood back, cracking his knuckles. 'King Kamehameha. The greatest chief in all of Hawaiian history, never found. Except that maybe he was. Maybe *you* found him, Kalani. At least, that's what you said.'

'Under torture, a man would say anything.' Kalani said.

'Let me put it this way,' the Rake's face loomed in Kalani's peripheral vision as he came closer. 'If you know where Kamehameha is buried, we can use you. If you don't—' he spread his hands. *'we can't.'*

Kalani understood the meaning. He understood it even better when the Rake started hitting him again. Blows to the ears, the neck and the temples stunned him. He could feel his own blood trickling to the floor, hear a great ringing sound, feel blinding pain.

And the Rake wasn't stopping.

Kalani felt blows to his chest, his ribs, his biceps. The Rake was just warming up. He didn't strike at Kalani's eyes or his mouth, didn't want to risk that, but the rest of Kalani's body seemed to be fair game.

Time passed. The Rake used him as a punching bag. Kalani couldn't take much more. What was he holding on for? Rescue? Did he have a stupid notion that Pierce and his new friends might come storming in at any moment, guns pounding, taking his enemies out left, right and centre like people did on the TV? Did he really have that notion?

Kalani, every moment, was being reminded that this was real life.

And real life could be brutal.

He tried to clear his swirling thoughts, tried to stop his head from spinning. All he wanted was for the Rake to let up, just for a minute, to give him a breather. But that wasn't happening. The Rake was systematically, steadily, beating him to death.

'Ready to talk?' he asked as he delivered another punch.

Kalani nodded. The Rake didn't even see the gesture. He kept on punching, enjoying himself. Kalani felt bruise on bruise, welt on welt. He tried to speak, but the Rake was having too much fun. It was only when the white suited man said something that the Rake blinked, turned away and regarded Kalani.

'We're gonna give you an hour,' he said. 'After that, you'll find that things get much worse. This will all feel like tickling compared to what we're gonna do to you. I hope you believe that, Kalani.'

The men withdrew from the room. Kalani sat in agony, wincing, gasping. He couldn't move an inch without sending a blinding lance of pain through his body.

Kalani knew he was done. No rescue was coming. He would tell them everything that he knew. And then, after they'd bled him dry for information, they would bleed him dry another way.

They would kill him.

CHAPTER THIRTY

Alicia didn't despair. She never did. They'd caught up to Kalani a few times already during this mission, and she knew they would do so again. It didn't matter that the 42K had him. She knew something that the 42K didn't.

Tom Pierce had a mole in their organisation.

Pierce had already told them he had an informant within the 42K. The helicopter that was abducting Kalani wasn't even out of sight before Pierce called that informant's number.

'I need to know where they're taking him,' Pierce snapped.

There was some whining on the other end of the line. A voice that didn't sound amenable. Pierce reminded the whiner that he owned him and could hurt him badly. He didn't want to have to do that.

The man stopped talking. A few moments passed. Then, a few words were spoken, and the call ended. Pierce turned to them.

'He'll come back to me.'

'Sounds like you and your informant aren't on the best of terms,' Russo said lightly.

'He owes me. I saved his life,' Pierce said. 'More than once. I could sink him where he stands. I don't want to but, right now, Kalani is more important.'

'Will they torture him?' Caitlyn asked with a wince.

Pierce nodded. 'They will get the information out of him any way they can. If we're not quick, we will lose Kalani and Kamehameha in quick succession.'

'Talking about losing something,' Crouch turned a quick 360 in the rows between pineapple plants. 'How the hell are we going to get to civilisation? We're in the middle of bloody nowhere.'

'Not that remote,' Pierce said. 'We still have cell reception here. Other areas are so remote that they do not. We can call an Uber.'

Alicia blinked at him 'You're kidding? Here?'

Pierce shrugged. 'Why not? They have Ubers at the airport. I have an account,' he took out his phone and started tapping away.

Crouch looked torn, as if on the one hand he couldn't stand the thought of the modern Uber taxi winding its way through the sacred, isolated country, but on the other glad for the easy way back to civilisation. Within a minute, Pierce told them he had an estimated time of arrival.

They waited at the side of the road. There were no more phone calls, no informants ringing Pierce back. The PI looked worried. He paced and kept on staring at his phone and sighed on more than one occasion. Alicia felt each passing minute like a death knell.

For poor old Kalani.

The Uber arrived, picked them up, and took them to Lanai City. There, Pierce arranged a boat, but he didn't know where he wanted to take it to yet. He was forced to put the craft on hold, haggle with its owner, wrangle a special deal. Still, he waited for the informant to call him back.

Nothing.

'All our eggs are literally in one basket,' Russo said. 'And they're scrambled. What about all your other contacts?'

Pierce spread his arms. 'They're all on the lookout. None of them have seen any known members of the 42K or Kalani on any island. It's as if the chopper just vanished into thin air between Lanai and Maui.'

'Or went straight to a ranch belonging to the 42K,' Crouch said. 'Which is more likely.'

With nothing more to do, and having not eaten in what Alicia felt were days, the team found a harbour café and piled in. Inside, the place was quiet, with only a few of the tables occupied. Muted conversation filled the air. They ordered bottled water and coffee and sandwiches, took two small tables by the window and devoured their meal with little chatter. Alicia couldn't recall the last time she'd eaten. By the time she had finished, she was still hungry, so ordered another round of sandwiches, which they shared. Time passed slowly. Pierce checked his watch constantly and kept flicking his eye towards his phone that lay between them on the table.

At last, it rang.

Pierce snatched it up. 'Yes?'

They could all hear the informant's tinny voice.

'It's closed shop here, brah,' the man said. 'If you're not involved, they don't want you to know nothing. Nothing! I'm stuck here in Oahu. Doesn't matter what other operations are happening; they tell us nothing.'

Pierce could understand the prudence of that. 'So he's not been taken back to the Oahu HQ?'

'That's a definite no. Look, Pierce, please, I really have to be quick here. They'll hear me and find out.'

'Then tell me something useful.'

The informant sighed heavily. 'All I know is they took him to Maui. There's a big operation going down in Maui, involving dozens of foot soldiers. That's everything I know, brah.'

Pierce nodded in satisfaction. 'That's good. So we know he's on Maui. *Where* on Maui?'

'I don't know.'

'What the—' Pierce exploded, then took a deep breath to steady himself. The PI was highly agitated. 'How can you not know?'

'I'm Oahu based. You know that. The 42K have operations on Maui and Kauai, but I'm not a part of them. I've never been. All I know is they took him to the ranch on Maui and they're gonna make him... talk.'

Pierce caught the hesitation. 'What else?' he asked.

'Talk... or they're gonna kill him. They've had enough.'

Pierce rubbed his tired eyes and ended the call. He looked up, biting his lower lip. 'You guys hear all that?'

They nodded. Alicia sipped her coffee, watching the PI. 'How about you, Michael?' she looked over at Crouch. 'Do you have contacts in Maui? Anyone at all who might be able to help?'

Even as Crouch shook his head, Pierce quickly spoke up. 'It won't do us any good. *I* have contacts in Maui. Good ones. Loyal ones. A fantastic mutual network. I help them, they help me. That's how it's always been. If they spotted Kalani, they'd call me. I... I don't know what else to do.'

Alicia felt a sinking feeling. 'So we're at a dead end?'

Pierce shook his head, eyes flicking left and right. 'I think so. My contacts have brought us this far, but... if they took Kalani directly to some quiet place, then they won't have seen him. The 42K have him now.'

Alicia watched the PI over the top of her coffee mug. He was devastated, unable to believe that he had lost. She looked at Crouch. Their leader, too, seemed at a loss. This, then, was their brick wall.

'What the hell are we supposed to do?' she asked.

The silence all around the table was deafening.

CHAPTER THIRTY ONE

Kalani waited and waited.

His whole body throbbed. When would they come back? He had nothing else to hold out for. Yes, he would tell them everything, hope they took him along on the search for the King, and then try to escape. If they found the treasure, so be it. At least he'd be alive for a little longer.

Eventually, Kalani fell asleep. He was exhausted, tired from the last few days of running and hiding. He'd had little rest, no decent food, and didn't have the means to stay fully off the grid. He was no hunter and besides; it was hardly possible in places like Oahu and Kauai. The entire world was made for living together these days, not apart.

He drifted. His eyes closed. It wasn't that he was relaxed; it was that he was completely spent. The beating had taken his last reserves of energy. Kalani fell asleep in the chair and found himself in another, even scarier, world.

He was in the dark woods, being chased. He was alone, in his boxer shorts, and he was feeling extremely vulnerable. Fallen branches and twigs cut his feet, tree limbs slashed at his knees and thighs as he passed between them. He was aware of something very scary and very large on his tail. He could hear it breathing through the dark, see the fog vapours that poured out of its wide, toothsome mouth.

Was it closing on him?

Kalani felt as if he'd been running for hours. He was slashed to ribbons, bleeding. His feet throbbed in agony. The terrible, amorphous thing was bearing down on him, flitting through the trees that were his only barrier, parting them as if it was made of smoke. He couldn't stand against it, couldn't hope to stop it.

It reached out for him with a nebulous claw.

Kalani woke bathed in sweat. It coated his forehead. His eyes snapped open, and it ran into them, making him blink. He was still tied to the chair in the same position. He was still alone. They hadn't come for him yet. That was good, because he couldn't hold out any more. He had the feeling, though, that the more time that passed, the better.

Pierce wouldn't stop looking for him.

And Pierce had a lot of good contacts. Kalani tried to stay hopeful, but the desperation of his plight made it hard.

There was a noise outside his door, something loud and brash. It brought the dream back, and he again saw himself pursued, cornered, hunted by something much bigger than him. He saw the doorknob turn and then the man with the white suit walked in, closely followed by the Rake. The two men stopped and locked the door behind them, and then turned to regard Kalani.

'He's coming along nicely,' the Rake said. The man's eyes were glassy, his face feral. The drugs were shooting through his system.

'Simmering in bruises,' White Suit laughed. 'Parboiled.'

The Rake stepped forward. 'You wanna cook some more, Kalani?' His face was wild.

The young thief shook his head. Even that small gesture hurt. He could see fine, he could talk fine, but the rest of him was one enormous bruise.

'I want to talk,' he said.

'You're kidding.' The Rake looked disappointed. 'We've barely gotten started yet. I've got plenty more I want to do with you.'

'Please. No more.'

The man in the white suit now stepped forward, taking centre stage. He bent down to Kalani's eye level and licked his lips.

'Where is Kamehameha?' he asked.

Kalani had been hoping for more time, for some protocol where a big boss had to be informed. But the man in the white suit, it seemed, was enough.

'I'll tell you,' Kalani said. 'But—'

'No, you won't,' the Rake interrupted surprisingly. He licked his lips, his eyes rolled, and he brought a silver Zippo lighter from his back pocket and then produced a tube of lighter fluid. 'First, I'm gonna burn you.' Sweat poured down the Rake's face in sheets.

White Suit frowned and held out a hand, but the Rake batted it away. His eyes were savage, his body language highly aggressive. Kalani saw instantly that he meant to do exactly what he said.

And so did White Suit. He backed away, called for backup.

The Rake was out of control. His face twisted. 'Just a minor burn,' he whispered. 'A shin, a calf, a thigh maybe. Just long enough to hear the sizzle, to start the cooking. It's the smell you see. I love it.'

The Rake came closer to him. Kalani went wild, struggling in the chair. He kicked out, wriggled left and right. He didn't want to get burned. His eyes flew to White Suit, who was banging on the door.

'Who the hell have you guys left me with in here? He's crazy. Get in here now!'

The Rake grinned. Sweat flew from his head. What the hell was he on? The 42K had made a big mistake sending a junkie to interrogate Kalani. He bent down close to Kalani's right knee, constantly flicking his lighter and waving the tube of fluid before Kalani's eyes. The door burst open; men rushed in pointing their guns. But, at first, they didn't know where to point them.

The Rake squeezed the tube of lighter fluid. Kalani saw the liquid arc through the air. It just missed his ankle. The lighter stayed on, flickering.

Kalani kicked out. He struck first the tube and then the lighter. Drops of liquid spattered the Rake's midriff and then the still-lit lighter fell on him. Suddenly, he was aflame. He went up in a woosh, a terrible sound unlike anything Kalani had heard before. Instantly, the Rake started screaming and staggering about.

He staggered straight into the man wearing the white suit.

And, incredibly, he still had his tube of lighter fluid clasped in one hand. He squirted it now, splattering White Suit and the gun-toting henchmen who'd dashed into the room. They paused, horrified, as the flaming Rake ran blindly into them.

The conflagration increased. Flames spread from White Suit to the gunmen. Screaming filled the air. Men collapsed to their knees and dropped their weapons to the floor. Kalani still struggled. The ropes that bound him were tight, but Kalani didn't care. This was the only chance he was ever going to get.

He wrenched and wrenched, tearing the flesh from his wrists. He bled, the blood starting to run freely. And that was a good thing. The blood made the ropes slick, made them twist away from each other. Kalani fought hard, pulling and pulling and forcing the ropes this way and that. He could feel them loosening.

Ahead, the men burned. Their screams tore at the air. Kalani couldn't hear anything but their shrieks, but had to assume other men would hear and come running. The Rake was on his knees, hands in the air, aflame but loving it. Even as he burned, he turned slowly towards Kalani.

It was a horrifying spectacle. Kalani's eyes were rooted, unable to tear away from the scene. The Rake mouthed something, blinked, and then fell to the floor.

Burning.

The gunmen were struggling, twisting left and right, their flesh crackling. White Suit was writhing, batting at his clothes and his hair. He shrugged out of the blazing jacket, wriggled out of the sizzling shirt. He fumbled at his belt; his bare arms burned.

Kalani couldn't stand the sight of it. If his hands had been free, he would have jumped unflinchingly to go help the man. All of them, in fact. He tugged and slid the ropes around, not feeling the pain, galvanised through terror and disgust and outright shock.

Finally, one rope loosened and fell free.

Kalani unhooked the rest of them, then bent and undid the ones that tied his ankles to the chair. It took him less than a minute. He rose to his feet, groaning in agony, the beating still fresh on his body. He looked around the room.

There was nowhere to go.

But there was *one* exit.

Kalani closed his eyes briefly. Bile rose in his throat. Something terrible gripped him, not just terror but revulsion and a feeling of cowardice. The men on the floor weren't screaming anymore; they were dead or very close.

Kalani approached the flaming mess. The only way around them was through them, through their melting bodies and charred limbs and sightless eyes. He had to look down at them to make sure he didn't step on them or fall into the flames. He gritted his teeth, curled his hands into fists, and stepped carefully around the Rake. Then, he approached White Suit, hearing the flesh still crackling, his nostrils filled with the abominable stench of cooked human flesh.

Kalani threaded his way between White Suit and two gunmen. He threw up. He bent down and grabbed a handgun that wasn't near the fire, slipped it into his waistband. At last, Kalani was on the other side of the carnage and was now faced with a simple choice.

Left or right.

He knew taking the right passage would lead him back the way he'd come, through the house, so he quickly took the left passage. The sounds of shouting were loud, getting louder. Many men were on their way. Judging by the sounds, Kalani figured he had seconds to get the hell out of there.

And when they saw what had happened, they would surely take revenge. None of them would believe the Rake did this.

Kalani ran as fast as he could. His stomach heaved, his forehead dripped sweat. His body was one massive ache. But he pushed himself harder than he ever had before.

Down the passage, where six doors stood to either side. Past them, all the way to the far end. Here, a kitchen sat to the right. More importantly, it was an unoccupied kitchen, and it had a back door.

Kalani lurched forwards, opened the door, and found himself outside. The one important thing he knew was that all the ranch's men were headed to that room. This was his window of opportunity.

The heat outside struck him like an open hand. He sucked up dry air. There were buildings everywhere, and vehicles and distant people working the fields. Kalani didn't like to think what they were working the fields for. This was clearly underhand, something to do with organised crime.

Kalani ran across an open patch of ground. The space between his shoulder blades twitched. Any second, he expected to hear a gunshot, feel a punch in the back, find himself eating dirt.

But it didn't happen.

Instead, he reached the first truck and jumped inside. He knew how to hot wire an ignition. He sat there for a moment, sweating, aching, gasping. It was then that the first stroke of good luck he could remember struck. Three trucks came bouncing down a rutted track, aiming for the exit to the farm. Kalani knew he would get no greater opportunity.

Quickly, he started the truck, rammed it into gear, and set off. The steering was heavy, the pedals stiff. The gears ground as he drove. But Kalani held on to the wheel and joined the little convoy, the last truck in line. Together, they exited the ranch.

It was stifling hot inside the truck. How was he for gas? Kalani checked and had a pleasant surprise – the tank was almost full.

What next? *Crap,* he thought. *What next, indeed?* He couldn't go anywhere alone because he couldn't live off the land. He needed provisions, and that's where all the problems started. What had he learned so far? Not to trust outsiders.

There was one last chance.

On the Big Island, Kalani had a friend. A great friend who would help hide him, who would share food and drink, who would help keep him out of sight. Kalani had already spoken to the guy, but had decided not to use him.

But now everything was different. Kalani's only other option was to contact Tom Pierce, but he didn't even have the dude's number. Yeah, they might meet up through mutual acquaintances, but that involved dragging more people into the mix.

And the Big Island was really where Kalani wanted to be right now.

It was kind of imperative to the whole Kamehameha quest.

The trucks roared along the road, closing in on Maui's central hub, which, Kalani assumed, was their ultimate destination. They hadn't veered from the road, nor had they slowed down, which meant that his presence had been accepted. Kalani wondered briefly what they were transporting.

Nothing good.

As he drove, he fished out his phone, checked the speed dial, and called a number. The phone was answered on the third ring. Not surprising since it was now early evening and his friend, Aiden, would be home whipping up a traditional mini-feast before trotting off to the Beach Tree Bar and Lounge for the evening.

'Yeah?' the man said. 'That you, Kalani? I thought you'd be calling.'

'I should have called sooner.'

'Damn right you should have. When should I expect you?'

Kalani suddenly breathed easier. 'You still working for the bus tour company?'

'Every damn day, man.'

'Good. I'll be there before you set off for work in the morning. And Aidan... ?'

'Yeah, man?'

'I have an awful lot to tell you.'

CHAPTER THIRTY TWO

Alicia fretted through the night.

At first, they'd been worried about Kalani and what might happen to him at the hands of the 42K. What was already happening to him. Then, through Pierce's informant, they heard the Kalani had somehow managed to escape their clutches and had vanished into the wind. Somehow, Kalani was still alive and well, and definitely kicking.

But that was where the information dried up. They stayed in the café for a while longer and then decided to find rooms, booking in to a local low-key hotel. The sunset blessed the western horizon with a furious display of fire and gold, something that lit the horizon from end to end and filled Alicia's heart with passion, and then it was fading, now burnished, now vanishing into the night. A strong wind rose from nowhere, racing along the dancing tops of the waves and battering the block building and the windows panes behind which they rested. After an evening meal, they all retired to a quiet lounge, Pierce always clutching his phone, anxiously waiting for it to ring.

The lounge was dimly lit, the golden wall lights flickering. They sat back on plush sofas, their feet out, and listened to the sound of the wind whistling through the eaves.

'What do you know of Kamehameha's funeral?' Alicia asked Caitlyn.

The young woman brightened. 'They buried him according to strict tradition,' she said, leaning forward. 'They call it the Hunakele and, essentially, it means that they bury the person in total secret, the location of his tomb never disclosed. Of course, this was all done for a reason.'

'To protect the king's great wealth of mana,' Pierce said.

'Exactly. Kamehameha had amassed a great deal of mana by the time he died. The Hawaiians would hide his body to make sure nobody ever desecrated it.'

'No clues where they took him?' Crouch asked.

'It's all very vague,' Caitlyn said. 'I mentioned already that they threw his flesh out to sea and made a special woven basket to contain his bones. The basket had mother-of-pearl eyes. Supposedly, one dark moonless night, they took the bones to a sea cave along the coast.'

'Which coast?' Russo asked.

Caitlyn shrugged. 'Not in the records.'

'Hawaii has an awful lot of coast,' Alicia said.

'Which is why they never found the king. It was said his location could only be reached by canoe at low tide, and that the path was fraught with danger. Deadly. A place where only the brave, or foolhardy, would dare to go. Even those that buried him only dared make the trip once.'

Alicia squirmed in her chair to make herself more comfortable and sipped at the tumbler of spiced rum she'd got from the bar. 'And I guess that's the place we're all supposed to go.'

'Of course,' Crouch said brightly.

'Great,' Alicia grumbled. 'Can't wait.'

As if in answer, the lights dimmed. Alicia looked up. A great gust of wind shook the building, and she fancied she could hear the waves pounding the shore not too far away. 'And why is Kamehameha so important to Hawaii?'

'Divine power,' Caitlyn said. 'Incredible mana given to him at birth and throughout his life. Not only that, but he brought to Hawaii one political system and the unification of the islands. He was known as Kamehameha the Great.'

Time slipped by. Alicia was as aware of it as much as she was aware of the crashing wind, of the trembling lights and the noise at the bar through closed double doors. She kept flicking glances at Pierce's phone, willing it to ring.

But by midnight, it was still inert.

The team didn't want to split, didn't want the night to end with no word about Kalani. But still nothing came through. Eventually, after one a.m., with the wind pounding the hotel like waves and the lights still dimming and golden and the rum still flowing, they called it a night. They went separately to their rooms, climbed into bed, and fell asleep.

Alicia was awake at 6.45 a.m. and headed back downstairs for breakfast. She hoped to find a happy, excited Tom Pierce already there, but the man sitting at the table, coffee in hand, a plate of bacon in front of him, looked glum and indifferent.

Alicia decided he needed cheering up. 'Sleep well? Dream of me?'

Pierce's face cracked a little. 'I always dream of you, Alicia.'

'Oh yeah?' she took a seat and poured coffee. 'What am I normally doing?'

'You wouldn't like to hear it out loud.'

'Hey, maybe I would. I'm a game girl. And I can take anything.'

Now Pierce looked more animated. 'Aren't you supposed to be spoken for?'

Alicia shrugged. 'Not sure I like that description. I'm in a relationship, a good one, but, hey, a girl can still flirt, can't she?'

Pierce looked dubious. 'Is your boyfriend a big guy?'

'That'd be telling, you dirty bastard.'

Pierce blinked for a while, then made a face. 'No, I didn't mean—'

Satisfied that she'd cheered the PI up, Alicia cast her glance around the room, spied Caitlyn and Russo headed for them and waved. The two waved back and then veered off towards the buffet. Alicia drank her coffee first.

It was 7.30 a.m. when Pierce's phone rang. At first, he glared at it in shock, but then he scooped it up, answering quickly.

'Hello?'

Alicia was just finishing her last slice of jam-covered toast off. Her heart was already racing. Beside her, Crouch, Caitlyn and Russo all leaned forward.

'I see,' Pierce said. 'Are you sure?'

He nodded a few more times, thanked the caller, and then ended the call. 'It's official,' he said. 'Kalani has reached the Big Island.'

'Isn't that Hawaii?' Caitlyn needed to keep things right in her head.

'Yeah, yeah, but to save confusion, all the islanders call it the Big Island. He's hooked up with an old friend called Aiden, who runs a tourist business. You know, ferrying tourists up to the volcano, waiting whilst they explore and then eat at the restaurant, that kind of thing. Aiden has a couple of coaches.'

'How can you be sure?' Crouch asked.

'My contact knows Aiden; lives right across the street. He recognised Kalani this morning as the two of them headed out for the day. Kalani is with Aiden on the coach.'

'Isn't that dangerous?' Russo asked.

'I guess Kalani feels that if he's with his friend, he's safe. Aiden is the face; Kalani stays behind the scenes. It's not like a tourist is gonna recognise him and call the 42K.'

'And what about your friend? Will *he* call the 42K?'

Pierce sighed. 'I'm paying him not to. It's tax deductible,' he added.

'According to the legends,' Caitlyn said. 'The Big Island is where Kamehameha was buried.'

'I feel like we're closing in,' Alicia said. 'If we can just get Kalani—'

'And hold on to him,' Russo put in.

'Yeah, if we can just get to Kalani and hold on to him, keep him away from the 42K, maybe we can complete this quest after all.'

'Kalani can't run forever,' Pierce said. 'And now, he's reached the end of the island chain.'

'One last chance,' Alicia said. 'One last push.' She rose to her feet.

'What are you all waiting for? Let's go do this.'

CHAPTER THIRTY THREE

The island of Hawaii, known as the Big Island, is the largest of the islands and contains some of Hawaii's most diverse terrains. It stands alone, embracing twelve separate climate zones, from coastal jungle to snowcapped peaks and houses only 13% of the islands' total population. Ancestral home of Kamehameha, it is also home to Mauna Loa, the largest volcano on earth, a volcano that has been erupting for the last 700,000 years.

They landed at Kona International airport late morning and made their way swiftly through the arrivals lounge. They hired a Chevrolet four-wheel-drive truck and made their way out of the airport and into the flow of traffic. As they drove, Caitlyn brought up Aiden's website on her phone.

'He has an office on Haleakala Highway from where he runs tours of Hilo and the volcanoes national park. Tour sets off at...' she checked her watch. 'Eight o'clock, so it's already well underway. I guess we should head for Mauna Loa.'

'The active volcano?' Alicia said dubiously.

'Yeah, don't worry. They have cafés and restaurants up there. Visitor centres. You name it. Mauna Loa is now perfectly safe,' Pierce said.

'Yeah, until it isn't,' Alicia said.

Pierce grinned. 'Absolutely right. But we tend to get some notice of that.'

'According to the schedule on the website,' Caitlyn went on. 'The tour group stops for lunch on top of Mauna Loa. So, if we hurry, we can intercept Kalani.'

Pierce asked Alicia to enter their destination into the inbuilt sat nav and then followed the directions. They rode up and away from Hilo, stopped briefly to grab water and sandwiches at a roadside café, and then continued as fast as the law would allow into the mountains. By the time they reached Mauna Loa, the sun was at its zenith; the brightness blinding even behind sunglasses. Traffic was thick, the roads full of tourists and locals making their way into the national park. Pierce crawled along in a snake of vehicles.

They parked on the rim of the volcano, sneaking their large truck in alongside a couple of smaller vehicles. Alicia noticed the separate coach park and counted the number of coaches.

'Too many,' she said. 'What was the name of Aiden's tour service?'

'Eruption tours,' Caitlyn said with a grimace.

'Right, well, let's head down there now.'

The parking area was busy, people bustling every which way, all loaded down with cameras on long straps, mobile phones, souvenir bags, takeaway sandwiches, caps and cardigans and backpacks. The team kept their heads down and hurried towards coach parking, trying not to stand out from the crowd. As they walked, Caitlyn studied the coaches.

'I can't see Eruption Tours anywhere.'

To their left sat a café, a queue out of the door, people sitting in seats outside and on the rim of the volcano. The ground there was black volcanic rock, cooled and hardened and comprising incredible swirls and churnings. People were wandering around the old lava flows, taking in the ambience and snapping pictures.

Alicia started walking along the rows of coaches, minivans, and old buses. They split up, taking a row each. Soon, Alicia had passed eight and then nine, and then...

She was face to face with Kalani.

The young thief blinked at her. His hair was wild, his eyes red rimmed with tiredness, his face puffy and bruised. His mouth fell open as Alicia nodded at him.

'How the hell?' he didn't say any more. Those words were enough.

'Aren't you supposed to be lying low?'

'I was never very good at that.'

'Ya think?' Alicia blurted. 'A fucking T-Rex could have hidden itself better around Hawaii than you.'

'But if you're here...' Kalani suddenly looked scared. 'They're gonna kill me if they catch me.'

Alicia was monitoring their peripheries. So far, nothing had changed. 'You mean the 42K?'

'Who else? I didn't kill anyone when I escaped, but they probably think I did. You can't let them catch me again.'

'You did well to escape,' Alicia praised him.

Kalani pointed at his face, indicated his body. 'They beat me up pretty badly first. They were ready to start the torture properly. To use fire. I was ready to give them everything.'

'But you didn't,' Alicia said. 'And now you're here. We can go dig up the king's old bones together.'

Kalani smiled at that, his face changing. Alicia saw Crouch and Caitlyn emerging between coaches up ahead. She waved. Kalani looked scared until he recognised them.

'What are you doing here?' Caitlyn asked.

'My friend owns a tour company.'

'Yes, yes, we know that. But why are you risking everything by showing your face in this tourist hotspot?'

Kalani sighed. 'I was supposed to stay in the coach. I just needed, you know, a comfort break.'

'Don't worry,' Crouch said. 'I think we beat the bad guys here.'

'But that doesn't mean they won't be coming,' Pierce said suddenly from behind Alicia. 'I can't guarantee my contacts won't inform the 42K.'

'Sorry to be the bearer of bad news.' Russo came up to them then. 'But I've been checking out the parking area. I saw some rough-looking dudes and they're searching for someone.'

'Are you sure?' Alicia asked.

'Of course not,' Russo replied. 'But I know vermin when I see it. And it's just too much of a coincidence.'

'We need to slip away,' Crouch said. 'If we can spirit Kalani away from here now, they'll have nothing to go on. It'll be the end of the trail for them.'

Alicia's adrenalin kicked in. She studied Kalani. The idiot wasn't even wearing a cap, nor a jacket. She wondered if they might go to the shop, buy some items to disguise him. She looked around for his coach.

'Can you hide for five minutes? We need to disguise you.'

'I guess. Aiden's coach is at the back of the row.'

'I'll take him,' Russo said.

Alicia nodded, glad the youth was in expert hands. She nodded at Crouch and Caitlyn and headed for the tourist shop. Pierce went with Kalani and Russo. Alicia slipped out from the rows of coaches and joined the flow of people again, keeping her eyes open for the bad guys.

She saw them almost immediately. There were two of them – no *four* – slipping in and out of the crowd. And if she could see four, she knew there were undoubtedly more. Someone had given up Kalani. Someone had blabbed.

And then it got worse.

Gunfire split the air.

CHAPTER THIRTY FOUR

Alicia ducked, but the gunshots were coming back from where they'd left Kalani and the others.

All around, people were standing still in shock, staring at each other, not yet ready to believe what they'd undoubtedly heard. The shots carried far across the mountain.

Alicia no longer had her weapon, and neither did Russo. She saw the four bad guys she'd already seen react to the gunshots and was the able to spot three more as they started running towards the sounds.

The crowd backed off. Alicia saw fear in many faces. Men and women pulled their children close. She set off at a sudden sprint, heading back towards the rows of coaches. It was a quick sprint, and soon she was threading her way among them. Ahead of her, at the other end, she saw three men with guns. At the moment, they were pointed up at the windows of a coach.

'If we have to come in there, we're gonna—'

It was the sound of one man shouting. Alicia closed in as quickly and silently as she could. Right then, the coach's windows exploded. At first, Alicia thought it was because a bullet had smashed them, but then she saw the figure of Russo diving out, suddenly airborne, and then coming down right on top of the three gun-toting assailants.

All four figures fell to the ground in a mess. Two guns went flying. Russo struck out, lashing one man across the face, another in the chest. Both men fell backwards, clutching their bodies.

The third man sat up. Pointed his gun at Russo.

Alicia was still running, but she wasn't yet close enough to help. Her heart skipped a beat. Then, another figure appeared, also flying out of the broken window. This was Pierce, diving head first. He landed atop the man with the gun and folded him in half just as he fired his weapon. The bullets smashed into the asphalt between his legs, his body folding with a scream. Pierce landed hard, rolled, and grabbed one of the spare guns.

The other he threw to Russo.

Nice moves, Alicia thought.

She closed in. Russo's eyes snapped to her, then cleared in recognition. He and Pierce rose to their feet. Alicia saw that Crouch and Caitlyn were right behind her.

'Time to get the fuck out of here,' Russo said.

'Where's Kalani?' Crouch asked.

Alicia felt a sinking feeling. 'The little bastard better not have run away again,' she growled.

'I'm here,' Kalani was peering through the coach's smashed window. 'Can we go now?'

Alicia scanned the scene, grabbed a discarded gun. They had seconds to decide where to go, seconds to make a choice that might cost them their lives. Kalani jumped clear of the coach. Alicia put him behind her and then ran to the end of the line, turned right, and peered from the back of a coach towards the parking area.

'What do you see?' Crouch asked.

There was no time to answer. The 42K were everywhere and obvious. Almost everyone else was running or ducking. The 42K were standing tall and all looking in one direction. Toward the coaches.

They didn't see Alicia as she ducked back into cover.

'Shit,' she said.

'How many?' Crouch asked.

'Too many. We need to run, not fight.'

The men they'd downed alongside the coaches were already coming too, groaning and holding their heads and torsos. Alicia knew she had to make a fast decision.

'Stay low,' she said. 'Look scared.'

They left the shelter of the coaches and entered the parking area. There was a lot of shouting and commotion, people were not sure which way they should run. Alicia and Kalani entered this chaos, keeping their heads low. The others followed, split up, and stayed behind Alicia.

And that was a problem.

Where am I going?

She had no coherent plan. She knew only that they had to escape the area. It was then that the line of cars filing out of the parking area grabbed her attention. Why couldn't they just drive out? *It's simple. Just like Russo.*

Alicia practically held her breath as she and Kalani threaded their way between cars, following other people as they raced left, right and centre through the parking area. She saw Kalani staring at two members of the 42K they were passing and forced his head to look in the other direction. She got a glimpse of the others following, staying low, staying among the flow of people, dashing right past the 42K.

It was a satisfying if nerve-wracking few minutes. Alicia reached the side of their truck and then realised she didn't have the keys. She pretended to peer into it, pulling Kalani close as if he was her boyfriend, hiding his face. At that moment, a 42K member appeared right in front of their car, studying faces.

Alicia stayed low.

The villain looked straight at her. Alicia hugged Kalani. The guy's eyes passed over her, but then came to rest right behind her.

'Hey,' he said. 'Tom Pierce?'

Alicia swore silently. Pierce had been pushing forward, knowing he had the truck keys in his pocket. Now, as he got close, the truck recognised the key, the automatic locks popped, and Alicia swung the door open.

She ushered Kalani inside.

Pierce was staring at the 42K guy as Crouch, Russo and Caitlyn flowed past him to either side.

Alicia climbed inside the truck, holding her breath. She knew what Russo would do. He approached the 42K guy from the side, hooked a big arm around the man's throat and then bore him to the ground. The two combatants vanished out of sight. The others took the opportunity to jump into the truck. Pierce settled behind the wheel and held his finger over the start button, ready to get going.

Seconds later, Russo reappeared. He looked perfectly normal, as if he'd just been out for an afternoon stroll rather than strangling a man into unconsciousness. He nodded at them through the window.

All good.

Pierce started the truck. Alicia didn't see the men watching Russo, didn't realise several 42K members had seen Russo take the man down, until they came running in from the right.

'They're coming!' Caitlyn yelled.

Pierce floored the accelerator pedal. The truck's wheels skidded in the gravel, throwing up sharp pedals, spattering the front of the car behind them. It lurched forward. The attackers flung themselves at it, trying to get hold of the door handles. Pierce hit the universal lock button, flung the wheel to the right.

The back end of the truck struck two men, sending them sprawling face-first into the gravel. Another had his knees cracked and collapsed in a heap. Alicia turned in her seat to get a better view. As they were left behind, the 42K were drawing their guns.

And the commotion was attracting more of them. Even with a quick glance, Alicia could count twenty of them in the parking area alone.

'I hope you know where you're going,' she said.

'Not a damn clue,' Pierce replied. 'I don't get out this way much.'

'I do,' Kalani said from the back seat. 'There are a few trails you can use.'

They flew across the gravel-strewn parking area, reaching a slight slope where it funnelled them through some gates and out onto the road. The 42K filled the rear-view mirror, guns waving.

'Go!' Alicia yelled.

'I'm in a traffic jam. I wish I could just hop over the car in front. I really do, but it ain't gonna happen.'

Alicia made sure her gun was at hand. They inched forward. The 42K got closer. Some of them veered off, running for their own vehicles. Alicia bit her lips. This was getting really bad, really fast. Now, Pierce was finally the lead car and put his foot down, slewing them off the gravel and out onto the road. One of the 42K threw his gun at them in frustration. Not the best move, but it clanged off their rear end, making everyone jump.

Pierce felt smooth asphalt beneath him and pushed the truck harder. Some of the 42K were also in their vehicles and following. They span out of the parking area too. Pierce pulled out, overtaking a slower car, ducking back in just before having a collision with a car coming the other way. Horns blared.

There were two cars on their tail. There might be more following, but they had to deal with the ones they could see. Alicia waited until one blasted up to their rear, just inches separating them, and aimed her gun out the back window.

'Down,' she said. 'Cover your ears. I guess we won't be getting our deposit back.'

She opened fire. Her bullet blasted apart their rear window and then the other car's front one. Glass shattered and flew everywhere, shards of it tumbling into the back seat and covering Russo's massive shoulder. Most importantly, the car behind swerved and almost ran off the road.

But not quite. Alicia saw the man in the passenger seat too late. He also had a gun and opened fire. The bullet fizzed past her head and smashed their own windscreen into tiny pieces. A harsh wind blew through the truck as Pierce fought to keep control.

With both vehicles slewing left and right, firing bullets that shattered glass and punched through bodywork, and with a third car roaring hard in pursuit, they raced across the rim of the volcano, surrounded by volcanic rock and smoke plumes where the rock had cracked, speeding through an otherworldly environment, each vehicle trying to outdo the other. Alicia fired three times. Her last bullet struck the driver of the pursuing car and made him twist at the wheel. The vehicle smashed hard into a barrier, spun, and flew across the road to hit a solid black wall. Metal crumpled. The car shuddered and concertinaed, bodies jerked every which way across the interior.

Alicia looked ahead. There was an empty road. She turned her attention back to the next car, which was several yards back, and aimed at the tyres. By the time her gun ran dry, she had perforated the front two, making the car run on its metal rims and slowing it down. Soon, it fell behind.

Alicia looked down at the four people crammed into the back seat.

'You can wake up now,' she said. 'Nap time's over.'

'It's about bloody time you stopped playing with them,' Russo grumbled, sitting up and brushing broken glass off his arm.

'Take the next left,' Kalani said quietly. 'I know a track we can use to get us off the grid. It's a big loop back to town.'

Pierce, face battered by warm winds, swung the wheel and followed Kalani's advice. Alicia took a moment to breathe, to relax, and then turned her attention to the young thief.

'You,' she said. 'Have a story to tell.'

CHAPTER THIRTY FIVE

Shunning civilisation for now, they all agreed to pull over somewhere in the Hawaiian wilderness and talk to Kalani.

Alicia did not know where they were, save from a red dot on a map. It pinpointed them several miles east of the visitor centre in an area where, on the map, the road was just tiny thin white lines. The terrain was open, studded with bristly trees and empty. Pierce had pulled off the road slightly, careful of the tyres and wheel rims, so they were slightly hidden by a couple of sparse trees. It wasn't ideal, but it was as good as they were going to get.

'What the hell is this all about?' Alicia asked.

Kalani sighed, flicking glass from his shoulder. 'I guess it's all about Kamehameha,' he said. 'Just like it's always been. You know the man is a legend. That nobody has ever discovered his remains is a blot on Hawaii's incredible landscape.'

'Which is where you come in,' Pierce said, turning in his seat.

'Yeah, that's right.'

'How can you be sure that it's Kamehameha?' Caitlyn asked.

'It has to be. The mother-of-pearl basket. The bones inside. The riches. The gold and the jewels. He's one of the most venerated figures from history, and is buried in the right place.'

'A sea cave?' Pierce asked.

Kalani nodded. 'Accessible from the sea only at low tide, I believe, but also accessible from above if you're... stupid enough.'

'Which you were,' Caitlyn said with a smile.

'I've explored these islands intimately for the last decade,' Kalani said with a shrug. 'I've done lots of crazy things. At first, this just seemed like another mad adventure. When you find some strange stairs out in the middle of nowhere, you follow them, right?'

Russo shook his head as if he didn't agree. Alicia knew she had that adventurous streak too and would probably do the same. 'But don't tell me you stumbled across these stairs by accident,' she said. 'Why were you there in the first place?'

'Now that's a good question,' Kalani said. 'I've always been fascinated by Hawaii, its legends and its past. You know,' he gestured at Pierce. 'That I disappear into the lands as often as I can, shunning people, shunning civilisation, hunting for... something,' he shook his head. 'I can't pin it down, but I'm driven. Driven to find something out there... a piece of me maybe, a piece of history perhaps. Or both. Maybe finding a slice of history will help me find myself and determine what the hell I'm supposed to do with my life.' He fell silent for several seconds before continuing. 'Anyway, I know all the old stories. I know them by heart. I've read the claims that his bones were secreted in the royal home of Kamehameha III, the legends of them buried in a grotto in Moku'ula, the more believable theory that they were buried in Maui's Iao valley, where many Hawaiian tribal chiefs were buried. I trusted none of these stories. There's a tale from 1984 of an old fisherman who, cast off course by a great storm, came close to the lava flow of Kilauea, the one that never stops pouring into the ocean. Understandably, the fisherman was scared, surrounded by plumes of white smoke and drifting ever closer to the bubbling lava. Desperate, he used his hands to paddle his way clear, though later he realised the ocean's temperature had left some scarring. It had even eaten one of his fingers to the bone. The fisherman then drifted around the coast away from Kilauea and, as the moon parted the clouds, found the hidden, ancient entrance to a sea cave. He drifted inside, but the pain was too much. Somehow, he had to get back to land and to his home. But he never forgot what he saw inside that old sea cave.'

'What was that?' Alicia and the others were rapt with attention.

'Nothing in particular,' Kalani surprised them by saying. 'But everything by suggestion. He saw a golden glow, a glittering light. It reflected off the burbling waters. It lit up the ceiling. He saw statues of discouragement, things left to ward off interlopers. Now, the fisherman was a traditional Hawaiian, a time-honoured man, and he heeded the warnings to the letter. He knew what he had found, and more importantly, he knew how necessary it was that the discovery was left alone. The fisherman left the sea cave behind, found his way home, and never returned. The only person he ever told about his find, before his death, was his son.'

Kalani took a breath and drank from a bottle of water. He looked expectantly at Alicia and the others.

'You?' Caitlyn said suddenly. '*You* are the son?'

'My father is long dead,' Kalani said. 'But his stories live on.'

'And you don't feel quite the same way that he did?' Russo asked.

'You mean leaving the discovery alone to preserve the ancient burial site? Not disturbing the cherished king's bones? Yes, of course. I've been struggling with the issue for many months. I only blurted it out when... when...' he fell silent, clearly remembering his torture at the hands of the 42K.

'I feel disgusted with myself,' he muttered.

'And now that they know, we *must* find the king,' Crouch said. 'Otherwise, they'll never stop hunting you down.'

'Where else can I go?' Kalani agreed. 'All I've ever known is Hawaii, the islands. And during the last week I've covered most of them, being betrayed by so-called friends. I can never escape the 42K.'

'Then let us help you find Kamehameha,' Crouch said. 'First, unlike your father, have you actually seen the chamber? The bones?'

'I already told you,' Kalani nodded. 'Everything inside the chamber relates right back to the stories we know of the king's burial. I mean, down to the last detail. And man, there's a lot of gold. It was always said that whoever found the king would become extremely wealthy.'

'We're not bothered about that,' Crouch said. 'We've found many treasures, and made sure they end up where they're supposed to be without taking a huge cut. King Kamehameha will be safe with us.'

'I'm beginning to understand that,' Kalani said.

'When you found the sea cave, did you have any climbing supplies? Anything at all?' Caitlyn asked, a discerning question, Alicia thought, as she looked at her companions right now. Their bedraggled state. Their lack of supplies. Their tiredness.

Kalani made a face. 'No,' he said. 'Though I should have. It's treacherous and the sea cave is, obviously, pitch black.'

'How fare is it from here?' Crouch asked.

Kalani leaned forward, looked at the sat nav screen that pinpointed their position, and then zoomed out so he could see Kilauea and the coast. He frowned. 'I'm guessing, ten miles, maybe fifteen, but you're gonna have to find Highway 11 to get close to it. No other road runs close, not even a navigable trail for a vehicle. That means looping back around via Hilo, which is going to take time. Once we're close, I can find my way back to the staircase. It's about three miles east of Kilauea.'

'Then it's settled.' Pierce said. 'We return to Hilo, grab supplies, and find Kalani's staircase tonight—'

'That won't work,' Kalani said. 'It's too treacherous. You'll never descend the staircase in the dark. You'll need all the light you can get.'

Alicia wasn't looking forward to this staircase at all. Not the way Kalani made it sound. 'Then we kip in the car,' she said. 'And start off on our treasure hunt at first light.'

Kalani nodded. 'That'll be much better.'

Alicia sat back as Pierce restarted the car and drove them back toward Hilo. They would have to stay out of sight, to blend in; they would even have to hire a new car under someone else's name. They couldn't take the Chevy back yet – the car hire place would be forced to report the damage to the police.

All they had to do was reach Hilo, and then start again, Alicia thought.

She sat back, excited about what tomorrow would bring.

CHAPTER THIRTY SIX

They bought flashlights and lanterns and torches, food and drink supplies, matches and rugged boots and backpacks and much more. They loaded it all into the back of their new rental – a white Dodge Ram pickup with four doors and a lot of space inside that had been rented under Caitlyn's name. She ticked the multiple driver's box and let Pierce drive, something the PI appeared to enjoy as he sat with his arm out the window, following Route 11 and whistling a quiet tune.

Alicia, in the passenger seat, turned to look at him. 'You seem happy.'

'Well, I'm sitting next to you. Life is good. What could be better?' The PI rubbed the bristles on his chin.

'Your flirting will get you nowhere. What's wrong, you're not used to lucking out?'

'It doesn't happen often,' Pierce admitted.

'Normally, when someone propositions me,' Alicia said. 'I teach them the error of their ways. But we need you along with us. Consider yourself lucky.'

'Oh, I do,' Pierce grinned sideways at her. 'I really do.'

Alicia looked away, smiling. Was she getting soft? As she'd told Pierce, when someone got overly ardent with her, their balls would be in big trouble, but she liked Pierce. If it wasn't for Drake back home... but she batted that thought away before it could develop. The fact was, she *was* with Drake.

So far, there'd been no sign of the 42K. Maybe they were keeping a low profile; maybe they were still scouring the volcanoes national park; maybe they'd quit and gone home. Alicia didn't know. She glanced at the others in the big back seat, four of them crammed into three seats, looking tight and uncomfortable.

The car climbed towards Kilauea. Sometimes they could see the sparkling ocean ahead, sometimes the terrain, and other times just stands of trees. They followed Kalani's directions as the day waned, as the sun started setting in the west, a flaming orange conflagration that lit up the whole of the sky. When darkness started falling, Kalani told Pierce that they were nearing the place he'd seen when he started on his own trek to the sea cave. Pierce found a place to park off the road and settled back, staring out of the wide windscreen into the gathering night.

'Bad timing,' he said. 'But best to wait.'

The journey had been steady up to now, hardly the beginning of a grand quest. But Alicia knew they had to find the right place from which to start. The traffic had been steady behind and in front of them all the way up, but now they saw and heard nothing for a while. Then, every so often, they heard the rumble of a car passing as it went on up the incline towards the summit of Kilauea.

They were sitting in a kind of lay-by, protected by trees on both sides. Alicia considered leaning her seat back, but then decided against it. She hated it when people did it on planes. Made her want to ram the damn headrest through the back of their skulls.

'Get some sleep if you can,' Pierce said. 'Tomorrow's gonna be a big day.'

'But we seem to have thrown the 42K off,' Alicia said. 'So not a deadly day.'

'We hope,' Russo rumbled.

Alicia jumped out of the car, opened the back door, and plucked out a bottle from their supplies. She grabbed a packet of paper cups too and climbed back in. The bottle was spiced rum, and she filled six cups before handing them out.

She raised a toast. 'To tomorrow,' she said.

'To Kamehameha and his bones,' Pierce said.

'To us,' Caitlyn said.

'To staying alive,' Russo said in a soft voice.

'Whatever happens tomorrow,' Crouch said. 'One way or another... we're ending this.'

CHAPTER THIRTY SEVEN

The next morning dawned in red fire.

Alicia hadn't really slept, just snoozed and listened to Russo's snoring. The big man himself could apparently sleep anywhere, in any position, and for as long as he wanted to. And just because he was able to do that, Alicia was annoyed at him.

She threw an empty paper cup that glanced off the end of his nose. Russo jumped and opened his eyes, startled, looking around.

'What was that?'

'Oh, you're awake,' Alicia said brightly. 'Just in time.'

Russo gazed at her with suspicion. The others all climbed out of the car into a cool dawn, flapping their arms and running up and down on the spot to stay warm and get some circulation in their limbs. Alicia followed suit, walking up and down the layby before stopping at the back of the car. When she felt slightly human again, she reached inside and plucked out a thick carrier bag.

'Breakfast is served,' she said.

They'd thought of everything. Even this morning's breakfast. They scarfed down locally made croissants and other pastries and drank cold coffee and bottles of water. When they'd finished, they pulled out their already packed rucksacks, shrugged them over their shoulders, and looked expectantly at Kalani.

'Lead the way,' Crouch said.

'Leading,' Kalani put his head down, crossed the main road, and started along a dusty trail. Alicia waited for Pierce to lock the car and then joined their little procession. It was already warm and she could tell it was going to be a hot day. There wasn't a cloud in the bluest of blue skies and the only blot on the landscape they could see was the ever-present rising smoke to the west of their current position, where Kilauea emptied its lava endlessly into the ocean.

Kalani didn't say much. The trail led them through a thick stand of trees, where it was cooler on their bare skin. Alicia shivered. Soon, though, they were out the other side and trekking along a wide path that twisted around a hill before plunging into a valley that Kalani said they had to cross.

'Are you okay?' Crouch asked him.

'We have to be careful here,' he said. 'The valley and some land to the south are owned by a local group of native Hawaiians who hate outsiders. Last time, I was able to creep through their land without issue.'

'Are they dangerous?' Pierce asked.

'They carry guns,' Kalani replied.

'Dangerous enough,' Alicia said. 'Stay low and stay silent. Kalani, let us know when we're through the worst.'

The young thief nodded and set off, wading through chest high foliage. They proceeded quietly and carefully, making no sudden movements. They couldn't hear anything except their own discreet footfalls, saw nothing except the endless greenery. After five minutes, Kalani pulled up and Alicia sniffed the air.

'Campfire,' she said.

'Barbecue,' Crouch said.

'They're roasting a Kahlua pig,' Kalani whispered. 'It's traditional. First you dig a really big hole, fill it with kindling, then stack river rocks on top of the wood. Soak the wood with lighter fluid and let the fire burn for a while. Then prep the pig. A double layer of banana leaves, soy sauce, brandy and five pounds of rock salt. Once the fire has died down and the rocks are red or white hot, flatten the surface, wrap the pig with leaves and tie it with wire. Place the pig in the pit and cover with more banana leaves and try to stanch any steam holes. Maybe put a tarp on top. Leave it for fifteen, sixteen hours and you're done. Man, it's as easy as that.'

Alicia was open-mouthed. 'Is it tastier than a microwave meal from Tesco's?'

'Oh, it's divine. I highly recommend luau pig before you leave the islands.'

Alicia didn't know what she'd expected of the terrain in this part of Hawaii, but it wasn't easy going. She felt like they were wading through the forest, the greenery up to her chest in parts, the trail almost impossible to follow. When they reached a valley floor, it was easier, but then they had the group of local Hawaiians to worry about.

They stayed low and quiet, taking a convoluted route around where Kalani said their camp was. Alicia thought about their dwindling weapons supply; guns were now held only by Pierce and Russo. Pierce had volunteered his up to the group, but they all trusted him by now, and had faith in his abilities, so let him keep it.

Alicia crossed green hills as they headed towards Kilauea, but remained miles distant. The thing they were headed for was actually the rugged sea coast. Alicia was ranging slightly to the right after picking what she thought was a slightly easier route when she came across the youth.

'Who the hell are you?' he growled in thick, accented English as he fingered a broadly bladed knife.

Alicia blinked rapidly. The youth had just appeared, camouflaged against the surrounding foliage. She hadn't even registered him until she'd almost walked into him, seated on the ground in the middle of the trail.

'Oh, hey,'

Shit. He must be one of the native group who hated outsiders.

'This is sacred land,' he spat at her and rose, holding his blade in a menacing fashion.

'Now hold your bloody horses, matey boy,' she said evenly. 'The first thing you want to do is stop waving that knife at me.'

The youth looked slightly confused, but seemed to get the general drift of her words. He stared at his knife, then at her.

'Sacred land,' he said again. 'You shouldn't be here.'

'I don't think so,' Alicia hadn't realised Caitlyn had come up near her left shoulder. 'We're far from Puu Loa, the site of twenty-three thousand ancient petroglyphs sixteen miles from Kilauea. Not near the temple, or *heiau*, built by Kamehameha when he sent his aunt to seek advice from the great prophet, Kapoukahi. And we're not near any other *heiau's* for that matter, and this isn't tribal lands. We're not trespassing.'

The youth twisted his face at her. 'This is our land. Sacred to us. You shouldn't be here.' He brandished the weapon.

'Now, look,' Alicia stepped forward, closer to the knife. 'There's only one thing I tolerate being waved in my face, and it's nothing as dangerous as a knife. So put it down before I make you eat it.'

The youth paused. He was black-haired and bare chested, and had marks on his skin that attested to him already being in several knife fights. This experience was probably what made him attack Alicia.

He thrust forward. The knife passed between her arm and ribs. She clamped it. Now, she could have seriously hurt the kid, but disarmed him instead and sent him falling back on his haunches. The kid looked shocked, glaring up at her angrily.

'What did you just do?'

'Saved your life. Now, scram.'

'Wait,' Kalani said from nearby. 'He could bring the whole group down on us.'

Alicia studied the kid, who looked like he was about to burst into tears. 'Look,' she said diplomatically. 'We're just passing through. Be gone in about half an hour. Could you please keep your mouth shut?'

The youth scrambled to his feet, eyes on his fallen knife. Alicia moved back to let him pick it up, which somewhat mollified him. 'I can't let this go unanswered,' he said. 'It's my duty as part of the clan. I won't let them down.'

'I saved your life,' Alicia told him. 'You owe me.'

The youth looked like he didn't know how to respond to that.

Then Pierce stepped forward. He had a wedge of paper in his hand. 'How much?' he asked.

The kid's whole demeanour changed, suddenly becoming incredibly receptive. Alicia smiled. Tom Pierce knew how to treat these people.

A few minutes later, they were on their way again. The youth seemed pleased enough once he had a handful of greenbacks, but they wouldn't rely on his good will. They pressed ahead harder, pounding their way through the trees and the brush and finally leaving the land of the locals far behind. Alicia sweated and panted and plucked her clothing and scratched where something small bit her. All the while, Kalani told them they were closing in on their goal.

'Can't you hear it?' he said after a long time.

Alicia was too busy staring at the road that lay before them. 'No, but I see something,' she said. 'Why the hell couldn't we have *driven* here?'

'You don't drive to a treasure hunt destination,' Kalani said with wide eyes. 'You slog through a jungle to get there, climb mountains, split rocks apart,' then he laughed to show he'd been joking. 'Seriously though, nobody can know we're here. And I didn't come this way. I don't drive. Lots of reasons.'

'What can you hear?' Caitlyn was listening intently.

'I'm surprised you can't hear it, but then I've always had acute hearing,' Kalani cupped a hand to his ear. 'The ocean,' he said. 'The sea. We're getting close.'

CHAPTER THIRTY EIGHT

At length, they came out of the thick greenery and onto a hard, black volcanic flow. They traversed this for a while, no trees before them, and found that they could see all the way to the ocean. Truth be told, it wasn't that far and, with every passing step, they came closer to their ultimate goal.

Alicia kept her eyes open, but it was hard to see anything in the landscape. An army could have followed them through the plants and trees and leaves and they wouldn't have been any the wiser. Anyone with a good pair of binocs could track them across this alien landscape, too. She'd been looking out for anomalies – as had been Russo and Crouch – but nothing had presented itself.

Maybe they were alone out here.

She walked on. The day grew brighter, hotter, harder to navigate. They stopped for a while out on the blackened lava, found a smooth area on which to sit, and opened their provisions. Alicia let her body rest as she ate pre-packed sandwiches and drank an entire bottle of water. She wiped her face, but didn't speak, conserving energy.

'The coast is less than half an hour away,' Kalani told them, standing. 'We will be there well before midday.'

'Is it cooler by the coast?' Caitlyn asked hopefully.

Kalani nodded. He led them away from their makeshift camp and toiled on towards the coast. To the far right, along the rugged rim, Alicia could again make out the point where Kilauea emptied its lava into the sea – the plumes of smoke rising high into the crystal blue skies.

'I hope you're ready for this,' Kalani said.

Alicia had been ready for days, but said nothing. She kept her eyes on the terrain, on their surroundings. She thought she'd seen movement at their backs just once, but it was too far away to be sure. They had a small pair of binoculars between them, but they weren't very powerful and offered nothing.

They walked on.

And then Kalani was slowing, ranging from side to side as if searching for something. Pierce was closest to him.

'You lost something?'

Kalani shrugged. 'We haven't come out at exactly the same point that I did months ago. And it's hard to remember. I'm looking for a marker.'

'What did you leave behind?' Alicia asked him with a touch of sarcasm. 'A rock?'

'I took stock of the land. Fixed positions in my head. I measured the steps from a volcanic feature. And yeah,' he admitted. 'I left a rock.'

Alicia winced. 'Shit.'

'Don't worry. I will find the feature. And then I will find the rock.'

They approached a trail that ran along the coast. It was winding and dusty, hard-packed. Alicia found she was approaching a range of cliffs and, before her, the glittering expanse of the blue sea stretched from horizon to horizon.

'We're here,' Pierce said.

'Not quite,' Russo said.

'He's working on it,' Crouch looked at Kalani who was still ranging along the edge of the cliff, looking back at the land.

'It's been a helluva journey,' Caitlyn said.

Alicia shielded her eyes from the glare of the shining ocean. 'You think he really knows where Kamehameha is buried?'

Pierce nodded at her. 'Have faith,' he said.

And right then, Kalani cried out. They all turned. Kalani was waving his hands at them, beckoning them across. They took a few minutes to walk to his side.

'Have you found something?' Crouch asked.

Kalani pointed inland. 'You see that distant cleft between hills there? And the swirling pattern in the rocks right here? You see that stand of trees, far off. And right here,' he turned. 'The way the cliffs make a double 'V' shape. See?' he walked a few steps. 'I should be able to find the rock in a minute.'

Alicia was impressed. Kalani swept the area with his feet, searching for the last marker. She stared back along the way they'd come.

'I wish I could be sure we weren't being followed,' she said tightly. 'But there's nothing we can do about it. The 42K could be out there, taking their time, seeing which way we go. I'm sure they have trackers capable of following our trail. They could wait and follow us into the cave. Once, I thought I saw movement.'

Crouch nodded. 'Me too. But there's nothing we can do at this point. We're literally *here*.' He looked excited to continue their quest, but then that was Michael Crouch all over. Put him within sniffing distance of gold and treasure and ancient artefacts, and he was like a lost puppy with only one goal in mind. Russo, on the other hand, was carefully studying the horizon.

'We have a couple of guns,' he said. 'We can make do.'

Alicia sighed at him. 'With sixteen bullets?'

'Actually, we can do better than that,' Pierce told them, his face speculative. 'I have an idea.'

'Something to do with your contacts?' Caitlyn asked.

'Everything to do with my contacts,' Pierce said. 'Now, give me some time and let me make my calls.'

They waited for Kalani and for Pierce, standing on the cliff edge with sea winds buffeting their faces. Alicia could hear the roar of the waves, hear the sea crashing into the rocks far below. The sound blocked everything else out. At one point, she fancied she could hear the distant hissing, steaming sound carrying on the wind, as Kilauea's lava hit the roiling seas, but knew that was just her imagination. It surely couldn't carry this far.

She lost count of the number of calls Pierce made, looked after him as he walked away and started pacing with his phone to his ear. She knew what he was doing and hoped that it would help them.

Finally, Kalani turned to them. 'The rock is here,' he said. 'Still here.'

Alicia took a deep breath as butterflies started inside her stomach. They were about to go find some buried treasure. It always hit her this way, the excitement, the anticipation. It was also a sign of the end of their quest.

'You sure?' she asked. She stepped to her left and leaned over the cliff, staring down a long rock face at the depths below. It was straight down, a rock-lined waterfall, all the way to a churning sea that smashed furiously against the rocks as if trying to break through. It was a constant battering, an incessant and unending rage that the cliffs always lost. Sea mist flowed up from below, gradually coating her face. The stark contrast of the serenity up here and the ferocity down below made her bite her lip.

'Be careful, Kalani,' Caitlyn suddenly said. 'You're getting really close to the edge of that cliff.'

And Kalani smiled as he turned towards the cliff, walked forward, and stepped right off.

CHAPTER THIRTY NINE

Alicia's mouth fell open. She raced as fast as she could towards the place where Kalani had stepped off the edge of the cliff.

'*Kalani!*' Caitlyn cried.

Crouch and Russo beat her to the place. Pierce was still talking on his phone and hadn't seen what happened.

Alicia stooped down to maintain a low centre of balance and peered out. What she saw amazed her.

'This is the staircase you were talking about?' Crouch asked.

From up top, it looked like Crouch was talking to himself. But from Alicia's viewpoint, she could make out a little more. Kalani had stepped off the cliff onto the first block of an ancient set of stairs that had been cut into the mountain. The stairs led down and down and were incredibly treacherous, poised right above the raging sea and falling at an acute angle, almost sixty degrees. Alicia understood that every time you took a step down, it would be like falling towards the swirling seas and an inevitable crushing death.

'You must be fucking kidding,' she said.

Kalani was looking up at them. 'It's the only way from land,' he said.

'What made you descend this shit in the first place?' Russo asked.

Kalani looked away. 'I guess it didn't matter what happened to me,' he said heavily. 'If the stairs stopped halfway, it would be terrifying, yes, but I'd just try to make my way back up. If they crumbled away, I'd be dead...'

'One little misstep,' Crouch said. 'One tiny mistake...'

'Isn't the treasure always worth the journey?' Pierce said from above them, his eyes twinkling.

'You finished with your hundreds of phone calls?' Alicia asked.

'All done.'

'Then you can go first.'

Alicia watched as Kalani started down the stairs, putting a foot out over the void, bending a knee and then stepping downward. It made her wince, made her stomach knot, and that was just watching someone else. Every step spelled death.

Next went Pierce. He took a deep breath, shouldered his backpack, and stepped out. His right foot came down on the first riser and then his second. He coughed gently, his muscles all tensed up. He pressed his hands back on the steps as if trying to hold himself in place and then he wavered slightly, rocking forward.

Alicia's heart leapt into her mouth, but Pierce was just stepping down another stair. He landed safely. Alicia took a hard, dry breath.

'Fuck me,' she said.

And she went next. The worst part was taking the step, trusting that you would lean out over certain death and then come down onto the next step. She took the first and then the second, shivering, shaking, not too proud to admit that she was terrified. On the second step, she leaned backwards against the rock, panting and puffing. She dared not look down, so she looked up, saw Russo above her. The big man looked about as scared as she was.

Another step, another heart-stopping moment. She could feel the spray fuming up the cliff now, washing upward from the violence below. The sound of the crashing waves resounded in her ears, the smell of the water filling her nostrils. Every nerve was alight, every sense hyper aware.

Alicia leaned out over the drop once more, let her body fall towards death, and came down on the next step. She repeated the process, taking it slow and steady, trying to get into some kind of rhythm. Still, she didn't dare look down, so had to hope that Pierce, below her, was moving at the same speed or a bit faster. The last thing she wanted to do was to bump into him.

On the fifth step, she had to stop for a breather. The problem was, Russo, the next in line, would come down from above and, if he also wasn't looking...

Alicia forced herself to move, pushing far beyond her limits. She leaned out, stepped down, felt the next step beneath her. The angle of the stairs improved ever so slightly, but not enough to allow her to relax. In a slow line, the six of them descended the cliff towards the seething ocean, coated in spray, their ears filled with the roaring waves, every step taking them closer and closer to the fuming waters.

As they descended, it occurred to Alicia that the way back, the way up, would be slightly easier. That helped her relax a little, but then the very thought of climbing these stairs made her bite her bottom lip until it bled. Then she realised that her focus was slipping. If she didn't concentrate fully now, she would die.

Alicia slipped down another step and then another. Once she almost struck Pierce as he descended before her; another time Russo almost bumped into her. Nobody was looking down. Everyone tried to descend at the same pace. There was a peculiar taste in Alicia's mouth, something utterly dry and parched mixed with salt. She tried to swallow, realised it was a lost cause, and carried on. At one point, it also occurred to her that their backpacks, secured to their shoulders, might sometimes be the only things counterbalancing their weight properly and keeping them safe.

And still they descended step by step down the ancient stone stairway. They didn't dare look up, nor down, but placed their boots inch by quivering inch down and down as if they were stepping into a trust fall.

It felt like hours. The minutes passed incredibly slowly. No one in their right minds would do this.

At last, Kalani stepped away from the staircase and onto a rocky plateau, shouted up to them to let them know he was safe. Alicia felt a massive surge of relief. It wasn't far now. She slipped down another stair, then another, then heard Pierce's great sigh of relief and, finally, chanced a look down.

Pierce was just below her, standing on a rocky outcrop.

She stepped gingerly down to join him, took several deep breaths, and then looked around them. The rock plateau extended about twenty feet in all directions, was hard against the cliff, and jutted out over the churning ocean for a few meters. They were that close to the ocean now that Alicia could see small waves lapping over the edge of the plateau, ripples of surf surging towards her.

One by one, the others arrived and let out long, pent-up breaths. Alicia gave the last man, Crouch, a few minutes to recover before turning to Kalani.

'That was one of the worst experiences of my life,' she told him. 'Where next?'

'Don't you see it?'

Alicia hadn't really looked, if she was being honest. Now she looked beyond Kalani to the cliff face. She blinked. Yes, there *was* something, but even from this distance, it was hard to make out.

There was a crease in the towering escarpment. Just a shadow. From the sea, it would appear to be another part of the cliff, a darker seam perhaps. They could only see the crease because of the angle from where they stood. And the crease, though even here appearing to be nothing but a wrinkle of rock, was actually a very narrow opening.

'Sea cave?' she asked.

'Kind of,' Kalani said. 'If you imagine, it's only accessible at low tide.'

'I don't need to imagine that,' Alicia said with a shiver. 'I've just risked my life above it.'

'That groove in the rock is the entrance to Kamehameha's tomb?' Caitlyn asked in awe. 'It makes sense. It's practically unnoticeable even from here. How did you know?'

Kalani shrugged. 'I didn't. I'm just nosey.'

Crouch grinned. 'All us treasure hunters are inquisitive,' he said. 'Curious. Interfering perhaps.'

Alicia looked up, way up, back towards the top of the cliff. The angle of the stairs allowed her to see straight up. The rim up there was ragged, angular and, for now, thankfully empty.

'All is good,' she said.

'Shall we continue?' Kalani said.

They moved out, walking across the rocky plateau, thankful to have the deadly descent behind them. The rock was slick and pitted, puddles dotted its expanse. A breeze rammed in off the ocean, plucking at their clothes and scouring their faces. Their walk was punctuated by the sound of crashing waves below the plateau, of surf smashing up over the edge of the rock. Spray drifted over them.

They approached the dark cleft. Kalani pointed out the way ahead, which wasn't really a trail, just a series of boulders. They picked their way between the boulders as carefully as they were able, stepping from jagged rock to rock, aware that a broken ankle down here would be deadly.

Soon, they passed through the wrinkle in the rock. The way ahead was unclear, just piles of rocks and puddles and heaps of broken-off rock. They followed Kalani out of the light and into the darkness, staying in an uneven line. They took a moment to unhook their backpacks and drag out their torches and lanterns.

Alicia held up a powerful torch, lighting the way ahead. The others followed suit. Their torch beams lit up the black walls. Inside, they could hear the dripping of water, but the roar of the waves was muffled now and becoming quieter the deeper they penetrated the cavern. They didn't let the terrain slow them, just picked their way between rocks, venturing deeper and deeper into the darkness.

It went on for a while. The six of them found a place to stop, to eat and drink surrounded by the damp atmosphere, the distant, stifled waters, the darkness that lauded over them like a protector, a spirit essence that safeguarded the last resting place of King Kamehameha.

'How much longer?' Crouch asked as they restarted their journey.

'Not far,' Kalani said. 'Your torches, lighting the way, will soon reveal our destination.'

At first, Alicia didn't understand. It was only twenty minutes later when Kalani's word started making sense. And then, right then, they made the most incredible sense.

'My God,' Crouch breathed. 'It's fantastic.'

CHAPTER FORTY

Alicia saw it ahead of her and held her breath, eyes wide. It was more astonishing than she could have imagined.

Their torches, shining on the ceiling of the cave and then reflecting onward, illuminated a brilliant glow of gold. It appeared out of nowhere, and the closer they got, the brighter it became.

It was a great golden radiance that burnished the cavern walls and ceiling as if painted there by the hands of old gods. It flickered in the sparse, wavering torchlight, glimmering and filling the entire cavern. Alicia was forced to turn away from it and pick a path between boulders, clambering over many and jumping down the other side, wondering if she and her team were the first ones to breach this place since Keopuolani and her friends worked together shortly after Kamehameha died.

If she closed her eyes for a moment, and used her imagination, she could almost see the ancient canoes nosing their war through the tumbling waters into the cavern loaded with their gold and jewels, carrying the bones of the great king. She could see the figures climbing out and onto dry land, reverently carrying the mother-of-pearl basket with the sacred remains, placing it in some distinguished alcove, away, always away from prying eyes.

Until now.

They picked their way closer and closer to the golden brilliance, climbing a short, steep slope, using the boulders to pull themselves along. At last, they stood atop the slope and peered down into the cave below.

Alicia found her breath taken away.

It was a stunning sight. There was a rock plinth in the centre, atop which a large basket had been placed. The basket gleamed in the torchlight, shimmering silver. All around the plinth, an abundance of treasure lay in ordered heaps. Golden ingots were stacked high. Necklaces and bracelets of all shapes and colours sparkled in between the glowing stacks. Rings and coins and spears, called *polulu,* and bows and traditional Hawaiian weapons like shark-toothed clubs and stone clubs and *pikoi*, which were tripping weapons, various daggers, throwing axes and javelins, all lay in state around the basket and the king's bones, signifying that the man who resided here had been a great warrior.

Alicia started making her way down the slope. Crouch pulled them up. 'Do we need to go further?' he asked. 'Or do we go back and call the authorities?'

'We have to confirm,' Caitlyn said.

'I'd say this is about as near to confirmation as we can get,' Crouch said.

Alicia didn't fancy climbing those stairs any time soon. 'Let's go deeper,' she said. 'We deserve it.'

They picked their way down the slope, touched the stacks of gold, wound between piles of jewels, and approached the great stone plinth. They stood as close to the basket as they thought they should get without being disrespectful. The mother-of-pearl had been fashioned into a face.

'See the teeth,' Caitlyn said. 'Those are Kamehameha's actual teeth, used to adorn the basket.'

Through small holes they could see old bones piled inside, covered in dust. Alicia looked around her at the gathered treasure.

'It certainly makes you think,' she said. 'All this veneration paid to one man, all this incredible admiration. I think we should leave now before we disturb something.'

They all nodded and picked their way through the piles of gold and jewels, heading back towards the sharp slope. Alicia climbed it steadily and carefully, conscious of all the slippery, jagged rock scattered around. It wasn't easy picking your way where there was no path.

She topped the slope first. The other side was a gentler descent, but still strewn with boulders. They crossed it with little conversation, all still feeling that glow, that sense of awe in finding the resting place of the great Kamehameha.

And then everything changed. Alicia could see the exit ahead, the narrow crease that led to the rocky plateau. From here, she could see through to the plateau...

... and she spotted the figures standing on it.

The figures ducked through the gap, into the cavern. They saw Alicia's group heading towards them between the rocks. At first, it wasn't obvious that it was the 42K but soon the men betrayed themselves by whipping out their guns, yelling and firing. All this time Alicia had been cursing the presence of the boulders. Now she embraced them.

She fell down beside one, kneeling and bent almost double. She peered around the side. Russo and Pierce had the guns and were moving forward to get better shots, picking their way between boulders and using larger ones to shield themselves. Alicia understood why they were doing it. At present, they only had sixteen shots between them. Not only did those shots have to be accurate, they had to be close to the men they wounded or killed to facilitate the seizing of their weapons.

She crept forward too, always wanting to be part of the action. The 42K members came forward, first two, then three, approaching through the small cleft in the rock. How had they found them? She had to assume they'd been followed.

Alicia had expected it. She'd tried to prevent it, but the 42K had probably been on them since the incident at the national park the day before. If not then, then when they'd visited Hilo. Whoever had been tailing them was very good.

But none of that mattered now. A bullet pinged off the rock close to her. She saw flurries of stone fly past her face. The 42K were coming recklessly. Neither Russo nor Pierce had opened fire yet, so maybe their enemy believed they had no guns.

Alicia moved closer to the exit, seeing more and more of the rocky plateau. It was right then that a body hammered down outside, making her wince. The wet slap echoed around the chamber, and a burst of blood exploded from the man's crushed head. Alicia screwed her face up. This guy clearly hadn't negotiated the stairs very well and had paid the ultimate price.

More of the 42K appeared in her eyeline, spreading out across the rocky outcrop outside the cave. She counted fifteen now. Some of them carried guns, other knives or hammers. They had come prepared. Russo and Pierce crept as close to them as they could get.

Gunshots echoed inside the cave. Bullets strafed the air. Three pinged close to Alicia. She looked backwards, saw Caitlyn and Crouch taking cover behind her. They were relatively safe behind the rocks, but they couldn't stay there forever.

Russo popped up then, like a massive meerkat from behind a rock. He fired twice; the bullets striking two men and sending them sprawling. Before the echo of the shots had died away, Pierce also surged up and opened fire. He fired three times, but hit only one target. Alicia heard Pierce swearing.

The 42K scattered and dived to cover. Alicia used the distraction to get even closer. Those on the plateau started inching their way towards the mouth of the cave.

And then it happened again. Another body fell from the staircase and smashed into the rock. But the 42K kept coming; they were being urged to get the hell down and find what they had come here to find. Alicia could hear the shouts of the bosses.

Back here, she could again hear the roar of the waves, see the surf rolling over the edge of the rocky outcrop. She found she was hiding behind the same rock as one of her enemies, only they were on different sides.

She crept around, making no sound, saw the man's boots sticking out, and launched herself atop his body. She secured the gun arm, broke it instantly, and watched the gun fall to the floor. Then she delivered three strikes to her victim's throat and one to his eyes. The man gurgled, went red, and died without uttering a word. Alicia reached down and took up his discarded gun.

Russo fired again. So did Pierce. There were two cries, two men thrown backwards. Alicia aimed her weapon towards the entrance of the cave.

Fired three shots.

They didn't hit anyone, but they did scatter everyone who was creeping around there. Some hit the deck, others ran to the sides or directly into the cave where the boulders were. Alicia used the uproar to creep forward past two more boulders.

She, Russo, and Pierce were all relatively close to the entrance now. She counted eleven 42K with more still descending the staircase. And of course, to her soldier's mindset, there was no better time to attack.

Whilst their enemy was vulnerable.

She dashed between boulders, a slinking assassin. She held her gun out, shooting one man who rose, wounding another. The cave entrance was steps away. Russo and Pierce were with her. Gunshots exploded inside the cave. Both Pierce and Russo snagged more guns as they ran, increasing their ammo supply. Alicia hit the entrance to the cave and whirled, expecting men to be standing to the right or left sides. There were none.

Only those standing before her.

She ran at them, panicking them. A bullet passed by her skull, close enough to make a humming sound. She shot one man in the chest who careened backwards, arms windmilling, before falling right off the rocky outcrop and into the raging seas below. She shot another who fell to his knees, her bullet taking the top of his head off. Russo and Pierce were also shooting, creating a wall of lead that took their enemies apart.

Alicia's momentum took her straight into one of the last of the 42K standing on the plateau. He dropped his gun. She smashed him across the top of the head, kicked him in the chest. He staggered back towards the edge of the outcrop, caught himself, and swung both fists at her. Alicia ducked, sidestepped, and hit him with a sidekick to the stomach. The guy folded, gasped., but he wasn't done. He fell to the floor on purpose, started crawling toward his gun.

Alicia kicked out again, this time hooking his body under her boot and sending him sailing right off the edge of the plateau. He screamed as he hit thin air, screamed all the way down to the death that waited below.

No time to waste. Alicia whirled towards the staircase, saw Pierce and Russo taking aim at the string of men climbing down. They targeted the lower ones first, knowing they were the most dangerous. Alicia saw a line of 42K reaching all the way to the top of the steps and more on the ridge above, waiting their turn. Or perhaps that was the bosses, urging their minions into terrible danger.

Pierce and Russo fired upwards. Their bullets struck descending men with guns in their hands. The men screamed and tumbled off the stairs, crashing down hard onto the rock plateau below.

Alicia ran around, scooping up the guns. She threw two to Russo, another to Pierce. She saved two for herself and looked up, a gun in each hand.

She was wild, focused. A bloody mist lay in front of her eyes, but it wasn't in her head. It was formed of spraying sea water and pools of blood spreading towards the edges. Pierce and Russo continued to pick off the 42K.

But they kept coming. They reached the plateau and charged. Alicia ran out of bullets, threw one of her guns at an advancing man. The weapon glanced off his head, brought him to his knees. Behind her, she sensed Crouch and Caitlyn running around, finding more guns. The 42K still descending had taken to standing or, in most cases, sitting on their respective stairs now and firing downwards. Bullets chipped the rock all around Alicia, barely missing her boots. She caught a gun thrown to her by Crouch, fired up at the stairs, pegged two men who then collapsed and fell from on high, plummeting down and squelching hard against the ungiving rock.

Pierce and Russo didn't give ground. But they couldn't do this forever. Alicia heard a loud grunt, saw Russo spin, and blood fountain from his shoulder. The big man was hit. His legs wavered, and he bent over, gripping the wound. Pierce yelled out as another bullet perforated the sleeve of his jacket.

They were in a winning, yet deadly, position. They were right where they needed to be, picking off the 42K as they descended the cliff, and yet they were out in the open, vulnerable to attack. Alicia saw two more of her enemies fall from the stairs as they descended too quickly, their bodies plunging together and smashing open against the ground below.

It was a crazy bloodbath. Russo was struggling, bent over, but still firing. Bullets churned the air up here as the waters churned it below. Waves crashed and boomed. Spray coated their faces. It was hellish, fighting in the thick of it with the beautiful, glittering waters to their immediate right.

But the 42K didn't stop coming. Alicia saw another bullet snag Russo, this one making a tramline in his left bicep. The man staggered again, but didn't go down. She tagged the guy who'd shot him, sending him off his perch and into thin air.

From above, bullets rained down. Alicia was ready to give the order to retreat to the caves, but that spelled an almost certain death sentence. It would allow the 42K to group down here, to come at them en masse.

And there would be no way out, no escape.

Alicia opened her mouth. And then Pierce suddenly gave a shout. At first, Alicia thought he'd been hit, but when she looked at him she saw him looking up, facing the top of the cliff and then pointing.

'They're here!' he yelled. 'They're here!'

Alicia frowned and looked up, too. Most of the 42K, spread out down the staircase, heard him and raised their heads.

It was as incredible as it was moving, as shocking as it was inspiring. Alicia knew Pierce had made dozens of calls earlier, but she wasn't sure exactly who he had made them to. She knew he was a man of many contacts, and now she saw what he could do with them.

Pierce had called every one of his friends. And he had told them why he needed them.

They had come out in their hundreds, and now they lined the entire cliff top, several rows deep. They held the 42K by their necks or their shirts or aimed guns at them. Alicia saw rows of figures up there, all looking down, some waving, some urging the 42K to climb back up under threat of weapons. Alicia figured she could see cops too, along with normal civilians, all standing together.

They had come to show respect for the greatest discovery of their lifetime.

249

Alicia breathed. She let out a deep sigh. She felt the empty guns fall from her fingers. Around her, the team sank to its knees, thankful to be alive, to be beyond the battle. As they watched, the rest of the 42K climbed up to the top of the cliff and waited to be chained or cuffed or simply arrested.

And then Pierce's phone rang. He smiled, scooped it out of his pocket, and answered brightly.

'Yeah?' he said.

'What do you have down there?' a voice asked, the voice Alicia would later hear belonged to the most significant authority figure on the island of Hawaii.

'You should come and see for yourself, though I don't recommend climbing down that staircase.'

'Stop being coy. Tell us what you found.'

'Is anyone else listening to this call?'

'No, my friend. It's just me.'

'Then I'll tell you,' Pierce said. 'It's everything I hinted it would be. When I called you, I couldn't be certain. Now... it's Kamehameha himself, surrounded by wealth. It's everything we hoped for.'

There was silence, as though the man Pierce was talking to couldn't quite believe what he was hearing. Then there came a single roar from up top, a bellow carried on the wind that spanned the entire coastline and the rocks below. It was one man's vented excitement.

'I'm calling in the helicopters,' at last came the reply. 'Can they land down there?'

'One at a time,' Crouch said.

'Are we bringing you up first?'

At that, Pierce laughed, and Crouch grinned. Even Russo, injured, shook his head.

'Not bloody likely,' Caitlyn said. 'You just try to remove us.'

Alicia had a caveat. 'So long as we go out by chopper,' she said. 'Now those I enjoy riding in all their shapes and forms, unlike those stairs that hang your ass out over hundreds of feet of death and pain and nothingness.'

The man up top agreed and ended the call. Alicia stared at her team and walked over to the injured Russo.

'How's it going?'

'It hurts.'

'Here, take your jacket off,' she reached out tenderly and inspected Russo's wound. The big man smiled at her.

'Is the arm falling off?'

'Almost,' she grinned. 'It's hanging by a string. No, don't, worry, it's a through and through. I can patch it up; go to the hospital later for proper medical attention.'

'That's what I was hoping.'

They stood around the plateau, coated by sea mist, surrounded by the bodies of those who sought to steal Kamehameha and had failed. Kalani looked incredibly relieved and intensely happy. Alicia saw the peace in the faces of all her friends and knew they'd done something special here, knew they'd made a difference. There was a certain satisfaction at the end of a hard quest, a feeling of fulfilment. And today, in the presence of Hawaiian greatness, in the last resting place of the great king, they had discharged any duty they might have to Hawaii's past, to the glorious tradition of the country. They had found, and then saved Kamehameha from his enemies, from those who sought to defile him.

Alicia felt proud of what they'd achieved. The Gold team, it seemed, had struck the bright seam again. Together, they had won the day. She felt justified, validated and, as the helicopters came in to land, she walked back into the cave entrance, turned around, and started smiling.

Her friends were all around her.

Ahead, there was a beautiful, shimmering horizon.

Which was where she wanted to be.

THE END

And here ends the sixth *Gold* book, where we follow Alicia Myles' *other* team's adventures. I hope you enjoyed reading it. Next up, it's more than likely going to be a new Relic Hunters novel in August.

If you enjoyed reading this book, please leave a rating or a review.

Other Books by David Leadbeater:

The Matt Drake Series
A constantly evolving, action-packed romp based in the
escapist action-adventure genre:

The Bones of Odin (Matt Drake #1)
The Blood King Conspiracy (Matt Drake #2)
The Gates of Hell (Matt Drake 3)
The Tomb of the Gods (Matt Drake #4)
Brothers in Arms (Matt Drake #5)
The Swords of Babylon (Matt Drake #6)
Blood Vengeance (Matt Drake #7)
Last Man Standing (Matt Drake #8)
The Plagues of Pandora (Matt Drake #9)
The Lost Kingdom (Matt Drake #10)
The Ghost Ships of Arizona (Matt Drake #11)
The Last Bazaar (Matt Drake #12)
The Edge of Armageddon (Matt Drake #13)
The Treasures of Saint Germain (Matt Drake #14)
Inca Kings (Matt Drake #15)
The Four Corners of the Earth (Matt Drake #16)
The Seven Seals of Egypt (Matt Drake #17)
Weapons of the Gods (Matt Drake #18)
The Blood King Legacy (Matt Drake #19)
Devil's Island (Matt Drake #20)
The Fabergé Heist (Matt Drake #21)
Four Sacred Treasures (Matt Drake #22)
The Sea Rats (Matt Drake #23)
Blood King Takedown (Matt Drake #24)
Devil's Junction (Matt Drake #25)
Voodoo soldiers (Matt Drake #26)

DAVID LEADBEATER

The Carnival of Curiosities (Matt Drake #27)
Theatre of War (Matt Drake #28)
Shattered Spear (Matt Drake #29)
Ghost Squadron (Matt Drake #30)
A Cold Day in Hell (Matt Drake #31)
The Winged Dagger (Matt Drake #32)
Two Minutes to Midnight (Matt Drake #33)

The Alicia Myles Series
Aztec Gold (Alicia Myles #1)
Crusader's Gold (Alicia Myles #2)
Caribbean Gold (Alicia Myles #3)
Chasing Gold (Alicia Myles #4)
Galleon's Gold (Alicia Myles #5)

The Torsten Dahl Thriller Series
Stand Your Ground (Dahl Thriller #1)

The Relic Hunters Series
The Relic Hunters (Relic Hunters #1)
The Atlantis Cipher (Relic Hunters #2)
The Amber Secret (Relic Hunters #3)
The Hostage Diamond (Relic Hunters #4)
The Rocks of Albion (Relic Hunters #5)
The Illuminati Sanctum (Relic Hunters #6)
The Illuminati Endgame (Relic Hunters #7)
The Atlantis Heist (Relic Hunters #8)
The City of a Thousand Ghosts (Relic Hunters #9)

The Joe Mason Series
The Vatican Secret (Joe Mason #1)
The Demon Code (Joe Mason #2)
The Midnight Conspiracy (Joe Mason #3)

The Rogue Series
Rogue (Book One)

The Disavowed Series:
The Razor's Edge (Disavowed #1)
In Harm's Way (Disavowed #2)
Threat Level: Red (Disavowed #3)

The Chosen Few Series
Chosen (The Chosen Trilogy #1)
Guardians (The Chosen Trilogy #2)
Heroes (The Chosen Trilogy #3)

Short Stories
Walking with Ghosts (A short story)
A Whispering of Ghosts (A short story)

All genuine comments are very welcome at:

davidleadbeater2011@hotmail.co.uk

Twitter: @dleadbeater2011

Visit David's website for the latest news and
information:
davidleadbeater.com

Printed in Great Britain
by Amazon